Incensed:
A San Francisco '70s Mystery

Charles Kerns

WhetWord Press
Oakland, California

In 1970s San Francisco, a long-haired, versifying student annoys his friend as they head to Family Day at the Lawrence Weapons Lab.

Off to the H-bomb L-A-B,
Where they keep the U-S free.
Free from hippies, free from scum,
Free from dopers, lots of fun

He bumbles into a bombing and hides out with a little help from his friends in an incense factory, a vets' hangout at City College, a commune up north, and a Tenderloin hotel, all while being tracked down by the FBI, Trotskyites, Maoists, and some new age lefties.

DEDICATION

To the incense workers of the world
To my friend, Paul Finnerty (wherever he is these days)
To PSA Airline that we miss so
To the Electronics Department and students of
City College of San Francisco
To Jack McCloskey, leader of the VVAW
To Eric Gildea, Patricia Zavattero, Andy Zeisman,
Patty Gallagher, Larry Linsky, Eric Zavattero, Ann Gilley
Francine Foltz, George Fuller, David Barr, Barbara Duckworth

and all who survived the '70s with me

To the San Francisco that was

And to my tobacco farming Grandaddy Allen

CONTENTS

ACKNOWLEDGMENTS

Thanks to Ghouse Salim Mohammed for the title

And to Eddie Grant, Marylou Arena, John Nash, and especially Dennis Evanosky for editing and suggestions

Finally, love and thanks to my wonder-wife Roshni who encouraged, gave ideas, and continually read through this bramble of local history elaborations.

SUNDAY

Sunday Noon

Off to the H-bomb L-A-B,
Where they keep the U-S free.
Free from hippies, free from scum,
Free from dopers, lots of fun.

Fred improvised his H-bomb song as his friend Paul drove them in a borrowed car toward the Livermore Lab in the hills west of San Francisco. As he sang, Fred bounced his head, his long hair and full beard flopping left and right, looking like a dog taking a joy ride. His voice only knew a few notes and had little rhythm, but he loved mouthing the words coming out. He would break into the lowest musical doggerel at any time. It kept him uninvited to parties and lost him girlfriends.

"Off to the H-bomb L-A-B…"

Paul interrupted, "I don't do bombs. The lab has jobs that do no evil, maybe even good, and today it's giving you the pleasure of an open house. So shut up and enjoy."

Paul put up with jabs about his work. Fred's songs never punched hard. "That's what friends are for," Fred said. "I witness your war crimes, so when the revolution comes, it's up against the wall…"

"But you'll still beg for a loan as you walk me to the firing squad."

Fred took a toke off his near dead joint. He offered it to Paul who shook his head. He didn't want the blur of pot that day. Fred decided a light haze was in order for what lay ahead. He started another ditty:

> *Nothing is as nasty*
> *as a duck-with-a-rhinoplasty*
> *in the morning,*
> *Nothing is as funky*
> *as an elephant sans trunky*
> *in the morning…*

"Glad you're back to your normal idiotic blather. Keep that up and you'll wear a straitjacket for dinner."

"And I'll wave to you over in the political wing."

Paul was thin, quick, well-trimmed, and myopic, while Fred was big, hairy, wide eyed, and a step or two slower. They both were vets: Paul had slogged through Vietnam; Fred lucked out with Germany. They had met when they returned stateside and hit the books. They shared rent on a place in the Mission, trading their GI Bill monies for a place to call home. Both studied to be techs. Paul had just graduated and was deciding how to spend his new paycheck from the Lab. Fred had another semester to go.

Their friendship was based on a shared cynical worldview after doing forced time wearing Uncle Sam's uniforms, but with differences in everything else. Fred was sloppy in thought, word, and deed. Paul valued precision and wanted the world to be logical in an A leads to B kind of way. He was a natural for the lab, but to get the job he had cut his hair and currently looked on the edge of respectable in clean loafers, ironed chinos, horn-rim glasses, and a blue, button-down shirt. Fred never worried about respectable—he lived shaggy and T-shirted with holes shining through—but for this day Paul had cleaned him up with a long-sleeved shirt and a new pair of pants, declaring him no more hippified than some of the scientists at the lab.

They turned off the freeway and headed toward the entrance where military guards checked IDs as cars pulled through the gate. "Welcome to Family Day, July 23, 1974," a sign proclaimed. Life-sized cutouts of mom, dad, two kids, and a smiling dog stood beside the entrance. Paul showed the badge that was hanging around his neck.

"That's me, Paul Kendzierski. And meet my family for the day, Mr. Fred Arnold."

The guard nodded, took down the names, and handed over a stick-on for Fred.

"Make sure he writes his name on the badge and wears

it at all times."

"Yes, sir." Paul snapped off a mock salute and drove through. They were in.

In the parking lot, children ran from their cars toward a newly installed ice cream stand where they lined for cones. In the heat, Fred thought ice cream was the thing to do and headed toward the line, walking past what he first thought were cone-shaped rocket sculptures lining the path. He bent down and read a nameplate, "Fat Man detonated Nagasaki Japan, August 1945." He didn't bother to read the others, the little atom ones or their big hydrogen brothers. Kids stood next to them, licking away. Some climbed them, yelling and licking their monster sugar cones.

Kids and cones,
Bombs and moans,
Radioactive
baby bones

Paul cut in before Fred could start singing a second verse in front of the guard in the walkway, then led him past the nearby labs heading for the Shiva Project. Fred loped along beside his friend's shorter, focused steps.

"You need to see where I work. Looks like a movie set."

"A horror flick, I assume."

"Let's see where you end up when you get a gig. Some free love, free electricity give-away, working for hugs and handouts, but no money—I see that in your future."

"I see big bucks, big cars, big women, and a monster burger every night."

Fred had not seen any of these in his recent life. Except for the monster eats. He zeroed in on any place that had a buffet after he got his GI Bill check each month.

They walked through the crowd, Paul in the lead, half wondering why he had brought Fred along to give him a hard time, but knowing he felt the same about bombs, only he couldn't say anything while still waiting for his security clearance. Maybe never.

"It's a good job. I'm not working on the Big One. It pays, enough for me to move to a decent apartment soon. It's interesting. And anyway, H-bombs are as American as hot dogs, banana creme pie, and the happy horse *scheisse* that plops down from Washington."

San Francisco was known for cold fog, but two valleys inland at the Lab, the summer climate rivaled that of deserts. That day, lab visitors wore sun hats and baseball caps. A few had umbrellas shading them from the sun, and some just sweated bare headed. Older bushy-haired scientists, most in ties, walked business-like and talked math equations, not paying much attention to the show. Crew-cut, forty-something technicians hung together, still reliving the Eisenhower '50s and talking military shop while their wives, most in sundresses and sandals, caught up on the latest babies and grandbabies and Good Housekeeping recipes. Kids played tag and ran circles around the scientists. Women workers, mostly admins, came in wearing their weekday dresses and heels. The black janitors and other bottom-tier staff had no day off and were on duty with brooms and garbage cans. New staff, young men like Paul, the just-hired twenty-somethings, almost-hippies toned down for their government jobs along with their less tame visiting friends, looked at the bomb exhibits. Many a "no fuckin' way" was heard from their ranks as they read project descriptions on the military side of the facility.

The lab was split into two types of projects, those the scientists said would save mankind and the others that would blow it up. Semi-hippies usually worked on the saving side where Paul's project was housed.

Paul abandoned his friend to do some serious jawing with his new boss after he got to the Shiva Building. Not sure how the boss felt about the hirsute wave taking over San Francisco, the group that Fred obviously came from, Paul went alone. In any case, Fred wanted to follow the more hippiesque bands of visitors to see what they did, but first he peeked in on Paul's Shiva works—a building filled with long, white steel arms jutting in all directions, aiming lasers at what looked like a pasta cooking pot. It was supposed to eventually provide for all human energy needs. Except for suntans and barbecue grills.

After ten minutes, Paul was still talking to his boss, so Fred moved on to the next building, a machine shop. It was clean, it sparkled, it looked ready for a white-glove inspection.

Cleanest metal shop I ever seen,
fancy tools looking oh so keen
for making bombs oh so-o-o mean,
All-stars of the war machine

Fred sang this as a C&W ode complete with southern twang and a clog dance. Then he saw the sign hanging by the door: PLUTONIUM SHOP.

> *Plutonium makes the bombs go bang,*
> *and kills in lots of ways.*
> *Inhale a tiny chunk, Fred,*
> *and you're so dead today.*

Fred was standing by a six-foot tall lathe and a ceiling-high drill press as he sang and realized that this was not the place to be. He held his breath, shut his eyes, and high-tailed it out through the nearest door, walking by the H-Bomb Employee of the Month Showcase dating back a decade with gold trophies shaped like the bomb sculptures he had seen outside.

He double-timed down the hall as far from the plutonium as he could get and reached for a door handle, but at that moment something went boom, then horns blared, sirens screamed, red lights flashed, and the door locked automatically. At first, he thought he had set off an alarm, but the sirens were everywhere. Something big was happening.

"Where am I? Dr. Strangelove's secret trysting place?"

He looked left and saw an open door far down yet another hall. He ran through the open doorway just before an electronic catch released and the door slammed shut behind him. This hall had offices, but no windows. It ran back twenty yards. No one seemed around. Only red lights and horns.

"Maybe some kid pushed the Big Button on Fat Bertha."

Maybe later there won't be
a San Francisco left for me,
But I won't care what comes to pass
The Big One's goin' to fry my ass.

Another boom and flash. The walls shook.

"It's happening, whatever it is. Maybe the SLA is on the attack. Or a hoard of hippies. And cops shoot hippies. And I look like a hippie. I'm dead."

Fred was not an optimist.

The stairs at the end of the hall only went up. Fred climbed. The next floor looked the same as the one below—no windows to escape through. The third floor up had daylight, but smoke filled the hall, and at the far end flames were coming through a doorway.

"I'm double dead—cooked and radiated—if I don't get out." He looked for a window, but the daylight came through unreachable skylights twenty feet overhead. The thick smoke curled down from the ceiling toward Fred and the floor.

He saw someone at the far end of the hallway, one of the wild-hair scientist types grabbing papers and notebooks from a safe and stashing them in a briefcase. He had a face like a half-shaved ferret, a look that went well with the bush of a hairdo on top of his head and the tweed suit he was wearing. Fred started to yell, but the smoke had blackened even more, and he decided to save his breath for breathing.

He dropped to the ground as he had learned back in Boy Scouts—Be Prepared for everything from hanks of rope all the way to A-bombs.

The ferret-face took off with his briefcase. He was either a scientist or one well-dressed hippie, Fred thought as he followed in a low crawl learned this time courtesy of the US Army.

"That dude probably knows how to get out of here."

He heard a crash. Ferret-Face had broken a window. Flames leapt up when a blast of outside air rushed in. A thump sounded when the man jumped through the dormer window onto the roof.

Fred upped his crawl speed—five yards to go—but glass was on the floor, so he slowed and stood, and as he reached the broken window, he saw a notebook lying there. Must have been dropped. Fred picked it up, kicked out more glass and climbed through to a ledge about fifty feet off the ground. Looking around he saw the ferret, tight-roping along the edge.

No one noticed Fred, or at least they made no offer to help, but he saw a way out. The roof intersected the hillside at a far corner of the building. Fred watched the ferret-man standing there, swinging his briefcase, then jumping to the ground, and starting to run.

Fred moved carefully along the edge—who knew where the fire was eating away underneath—and finally when the roof was a foot from the hillside, he jumped onto the grass near where the ferret-face had landed.

Fred looked down the hill toward the lower floors and saw guards rounding up the visitors and moving them to a far parking lot.

Flames on high,
Cops below
That's not where
I'm gonna go.

He ran over the hill toward the front gate, tucking the notebook he had found, one of those small, bound, black ones like he used for his electronics lab class, into the back of his jeans next to skin. Fred liked things simple—no briefcase, no backpack. Nothing but pants and meat underneath. Paul would remind him it's not socially acceptable to pull a book out of your ass, but social sins were acceptable in the circles Fred ran in.

"I was crazy to go with Paul and see this bomb factory. I am out of here."

The lab was fenced but fire trucks and ambulances rushed in through the gate. In the confusion, Fred squeezed out when a line of green government trucks entered. Ten minutes later, he stood at the freeway, thumb out—who cared if hitchhiking was illegal on the freeway. A beat up, '50s pickup with two longhairs stopped.

"What's happening, dude. They chasing you?"

These two wouldn't notice if cops were right behind them. Their wide-open-pupils stared at the flashing lights going by toward the lab.

"I don't know what happened. Just trying to get to the city."

"Trippy. Climb in back, the dogs won't kill you, but the fleas just might.

Sunday Evening

> *Fleas jumped high, fleas jumped low,*
> *Leaving their dog, Rover.*
> *I killed two, but they bit me*
> *More than ten times over.*
> *Life is fair, that is what!*
> *Justice just like Moses's.*
> *They are dead and I'm not*
> *And with this song you knows-es.*

Fred had jumped out of the pickup after it crossed the bridge, walked five miles to his apartment, and was singing in the shower, soaping hard to get off the smoke and sweat and dog hair. Paul got back while Fred was soaping and heard the news about the lab blaring on the radio. Fred didn't want to hear. He continued singing loud as he could about dying fleas, trying to keep his brain busy and his ears occupied. He dried, pulled on a clean pair and a tee, and walked barefoot out the bathroom door. His dirty jeans, shirt, and the lab notebook lay in a pile by his desk.

Paul, still in his jacket, stood in the hallway waiting.

"Are you coming out, Fred?"

Fred barefooted into the hall.

"Paul, you made it out of the lab. Congratulations."

"I was always OK. You were the one in question. Someone said a hippie guy that sounded like you was in the building that burned, and they thought you got toasted, you bought it in the explosion, but I had faith in your serendipitous stupidity but mostly in your luck. Stupidity got you out of the place and left me in a pile of… "

"They think I'm dead?"

"Life would be simpler if you were. In fact, I should do the deed myself. You left me to face the cops. You were the only one missing when they counted noses, and somehow, they blamed me for it. They finally let me go, but I answered an hour of questions about you, my family for the day. They think you might be dead or might be one of the bombers or maybe both."

"Me?"

"I was writing your obit as I crossed the Bridge. 'Nice Irish boy, loved his mom, his girl Rhonda, and the city's sleazier hamburger joints. Mr. Fred Arnold died today leading the revolution to free Livermore…'"

Fred cut him off, "The cops want me?"

"I got a number for you to call. I told them you didn't blow up the place. Don't know if I convinced them, but they had a dog sniff my car and my leg, and both passed bomb inspection."

"Christ, I just wanted to go home. And get cleaned up. And eat something. I still haven't."

"Have you been listening to me. The cops. They're after you. Don't tell me you were there when they blew the place up, and all you can think about is food."

Fred with his wild beard and his "Do it in the Street" tee shirt might look like a danger to society, but he was more of a danger to himself. In danger of too many donuts and burgers most of all. He liked to say the world was changing all by itself without any help from him.

I like to watch and try to catch a little of what's cooking.
The world, it turns. The world it burns, but I am only looking.

"Blow it up? Do I look crazy?"

Paul shrugged his shoulders. "We could all be crazies. That's what San Francisco is about."

I'm a-walking Mission Street
wanting something big to eat.
But Paul, he wants a me to confess,
I want a burger. YES YES YES.

Fred and Paul walked from their apartment heading for Mission. They turned and walked passing storefronts looking like those Fred remembered from his grade school, all-American Main Street days of the '50's, but here in this part of San Francisco, large hand-painted signs with doubly marked-down prices said this was a land of the poor. They passed Spanish-only shops that sold everything anyone needed at half the price of the all-white stores a mile away. Sometimes the clothes did not last as long or pots and pans were thinner, or the suitcases and bags were in strange colors to Fred's white suburban sensibilities, but that never kept him away.

They passed Spanish-speaking families heading to the dime store and then they passed bars and finally got to the Chat and Chew, a restaurant that had opened back when the Mission District was Irish. Old timers, shriveled, and shrunken like retired leprechauns, still returned when the bars opened at 6 a.m.

They entered the Chew, a greasy spoon with a linoleum-covered counter, six wooden booths, two big drip coffeemakers, and a grill that had watched tons of burgers offering up their blood, gristle, and grease to the patrons.

Paul took a booth.

"I'm sorry about leaving you, and you getting dog-sniffed, but first things first." Fred ordered a double cheese with bacon, Paul went basic burger with a catsup, mustard, and pickle trifecta. They both ate too fast for conversation. Fred dripped rare juices; Paul kept it clean with a pile of extra napkins.

"Next course?" Fred asked as he dropped four quarters on the table to cover his half of the bill.

"As always." Paul bowed and laid down a dollar.

They followed their normal routine and moved next door to Donut Heaven shining in its full chrome-plated glory, complemented with orange vinyl stools and a pink Formica counter. All it had in common with the Chew was high-acid, watered-down coffee and the same worn-down patrons.

Fred called for a pair of deep-fried old-fashioneds with a twenty-ounce coffee worthy of an avowed dunker; Paul ordered two glazed holes but went dry—he always held out for espresso up in North Beach, gagging at the south of Market brew.

They started their daily routine, "How can you swallow that Bun-o-Matic dribble? That Maxwell House footwash?"

"Just like my mother made," Fred dunked, chomped, slurped his reply, and then chugged the cup, plowing through the glazed sheen on top and crumbs on the bottom.

"OK, what really happened at the lab?"

"I don't know what happened. I just ran out knowing I didn't belong there and hitchhiked home and got hungry. That's the story. What I'll tell the cops when I see them."

"Are you sure? Someone saw you in the building. Remember when I got you out of trouble before? I'm here if you need help when you turn yourself in. I'm your proto-lawyer-in-waiting any time you want."

It had been six months since Fred was holding the shoebox full of stems and seeds, cleaning them to make one last joint, when he yelled "come on up" after the doorbell rang. Two cops, guns out, double-stepped the stairs and kept on to the back window, looking out into the jungle of a back yard. Paul grabbed Fred's shoebox and managed to stash everything in the refrigerator. He pulled out a loaf of seedy new age bread and a jar of peanut butter, spreading it on thick, filling the room with that oily, sticky smell that only a six-year-old could love. Fred looked bug-eyed at the cops when they turned back to look in the kitchen. Paul shoved the oily bread toward Fred's mouth and did a who-me, pussycat grin.

"Reports of prowlers in the neighbor's yard, sirs." The cops looked around the kitchen as they spoke. Their guns had gone home to their holsters.

"No prowlers here, just us simple city folks having lunch."

"Mind if we look around?"

Paul gave a guided tour: his room full of books and his typewriting table, Fred's with its electronics bench and circuit boards, the living room with old furniture draped with Indian bedspreads. Incense sticks had burned down to bare bamboo nubs and stood askew in an ashtray by the stereo. The cops left shaking their heads, talking about hippie trash as they slammed the door.

"I saved your ass back then," Paul said.

"So, what happened to you at the lab?" Fred changed the flow of the conversation and looked toward Paul. "Were you near the explosion?"

"I saw nothing, heard nothing, and said nothing. OK, I heard the boom. I was in the Shiva Lab with my boss when it blew. They rounded us up and started asking questions. I said I came with my friend Fred and then they started counting noses. Yours was gone, so I got sent to the bad boys' room. Finally, the dogs sniffed me over, and they let me go home."

"Then, there's nothing to explain to the cops. You saw nothing. I saw nothing."

"But you ran away. You need to clear that up."

"Maybe they'll catch someone quick and forget me. You know I have an aversion to blue. They'll want to grill me more than a burger"

"You've got to see them. Cops'll never forget you. They're the elephants of San Francisco. And not the ones you see at the zoo. They stomp down huts and throw villagers in the air, so get this cleared up before they go on the rampage. Remember I can get hit with friendly fire if you don't. Call them." Paul liked to keep his nose clean. And his friends' noses, too. Especially when he had his new goldmine of a job.

Fred looked at the shelf of donuts and then at his friend. "I'll call tomorrow. I'm going to work now. Give me the police number. I definitely will call them tomorrow"

Paul copied the cops' number on a napkin. Fred took it and walked away, singing louder than usual, drawing looks from the shoppers who were used to crazies but not singing ones.

I did the H-bomb dance today
And I barely got away
Now I'm happy to be free
Kiss the cops goodnight for me

He had meant to tell Paul about getting lost and the ferret-face and the notebook and climbing through the building window, but it was better to keep quiet. Anyway, the notebook would fit nicely into a trash can. That would end the story quickly.

Sunday Night

The smell of watermelon knocked you down, but Fred's nose had numbed after six months on the job. He loaded a tray with plain joss sticks imported by the ton from India, dunked the tray into a fifty-gallon drum filled halfway with man-made, artificial watermelon oil. He hung the tray on top of the drum for the sticks packed inside to drip and dry. Watermelon—done. Next up, vanilla, then patchouli, then cherry. The vanilla drum was low, so he opened a 10 gallon can of synthetic oil, straight from Dow—Dow was an Incense Company secret in those days of napalm and burning babies.

> *I make incense way past dusk*
> *Patchouli, lemon, cherry, musk.*
> *Burn a stick and smoke some dope*
> *Turn up the music, life's got hope.*

The room was filled with stacks of boxes, all loaded with dipped incense sticks ready for packing into cardboard sleeves, the kind you found hanging in your local head shop. Incense was a good business: a tenth of a penny's worth of incense cost a dollar at the store. The cardboard package cost, at most, two cents, and labor was another three. So what if half the head shops went broke and never paid in full? It only took a few paying survivors to make the business fly. Fred understood the business, but the owner made the money. Fred was happy, though, with his minimum wage and freedom to work any hours he wanted as long as the incense was ready when the packers needed it. He had one more semester of part-timing before graduation and a decent electronics job like Paul. Not in bombs, though, maybe something with those new little calculators—they were far out.

> *I make incense that does smell*
> *Not quite with the stench of hell.*
> *Aroma of some angel skin*
> *Is not what I dump my sticks in.*
> *Dow Industries is at the core*
> *Of what hippies sniff and then abhor.*

He liked working nights when it was quiet. He sang to keep it quiet in his head but then he started thinking about cops and the notebook. That lead to another song with a stronger beat:

> *I gotta dump it. Whump Whump*
> *Shouldn't uh grabbed it. Whump Whump*
> *I gotta dump it. Whump Whump*
> *Where's a trash truck? Whump Whump*

"Dump what? Some of that crap incense?" A young woman stuck her head through the door into the incense room.

Rhonda was Fred's part-time squeeze. That's what Paul called her. Fred didn't want anyone else, but she was wondering. Fred had become habit-forming in the three months they had been together. She wanted to make sure he wasn't harmful, or worse, simply time consuming.

She had figured out Fred was your basic human guy, fun sometimes, sometimes a pain, and probably no more than an interim partner, unfortunately one with a quirk, his on and off singing blather that she had hoped to squelch but now was wondering if turning him off was possible. Maybe he could be an investment, one to be housebroken, but currently he was lost in space, waiting to see who he was. He had given her a key to the incense factory, and she surprised him once or twice a week. Enough for her basic man needs. Enough so it wasn't a surprise anymore—enough to be a habit.

"Want dinner? You get to treat," Rhonda said.

"I'll treat but I got a thing for Doggie Diner."

He walked over and started to give her a hug, but she backed away.

"You're fully incensed again. No hugs until you wash that evil smell away."

Fred unpacked his chilli cheesedogs. Rhonda had balked at everything on the Dog's menu. She made herself an omelet with a slice of ham on top, cut from a ten-pound present from Paul's mom that he was sharing with Fred in the interests of roommate solidarity and of clearing space in the fridge. Fred poured a glass of Gallo from his gallon jug on the table; Rhonda stuck with H_2O tap. Paul was still out with his ladyfriend, or Rhonda would have had cheese on her omelet. She couldn't just take cheese. Fred had already chewed his way through his share of the week's shared cheddar chunk, and Paul was sensitive about excessive cheese theft.

"OK, what are you going to 'Dump, Whump Whump?'" Rhonda asked remembering his ditty from the factory. After wiping the chili from his chin, Fred decided it was time to tell all.

"I've got this notebook, and it's from the lab that blew up today."

She nodded and returned to her egg. She knew that pushing him for details would clam him shut, but also knew he would burst out with a song or story if you left him on simmer. She went back to her egg and ham.

"I wandered into the plutonium room and ran out of that place. You know what it does. I got lost and the first explosion happened and the sirens and lights…"

"I told you not to go."

The rest of the story tumbled out. Rhonda had shaken her head at the word plutonium, laughed when Ferret-Face appeared, and rolled her eyes when Fred picked up the notebook in front of the broken window.

"I told you the lab was toxic, but you had to go see. Now let's find out what's in that notebook of yours. Probably something that will kill you faster than plutonium."

Rhonda saw the lab as betrayal. It was run by the university in Berkeley where she had studied and learned to protest, where she had swallowed her share of undergrad tear gas and chanted with the best of them. And her school, the one she loved, was running the lab, making bombs.

Fred headed into his room for the notebook. Rhonda took the final bite of her omelet and sipped at his Gallo but spit the vile, bottom-of-the-barrel wine into a napkin.

Rhonda was a no-nonsense, practical woman, twenty-two, short and chunky in a cute sort of way, with black hair cut near shoulder length, dark eyes, and exaggerated cheeks that would push her into a smile even when she didn't want one. She and Fred made a memorable couple with him towering over her while she guided the ditty-singing dreamer, so he didn't wander off in the wrong direction.

They had been a couple for three months, starting with nights together and never getting much beyond meals and movies and bedtime. Friends gave the Fred-Rhonda connection little chance, but Fred didn't know that. Rhonda did, however, and had been thinking of what lay ahead—more Fred and Fred's not quite clean sheets and mind-numbing ditties. She hoped she could wait until he finished school, got a real job out of the incense business, and smelled human, not like a flower and fruit market. Then she would see who he was.

She had come to the incense factory after work, after taking orders and cleaning tables at the Owl and Monkey, a relaxed hippie sandwich hangout in the Sunset, near the park she loved. Like most recent arrivals from around the country, she was a part timer figuring out where she was heading. The Owl and Monkey was no more than a short stopover in her life, one to pay the rent.

She wore her normal outfit, jeans and a tee, what everyone wore in the city, and had hung the wool shirt she used as a jacket on the back of the chair. She was a basic 1970's San Franciscan, just as Fred was the male version of the species.

Fred laid the notebook on the table. He hadn't looked inside yet but was interested. He could throw it away after they did a quick check. Rhonda grabbed and started paging through.

"Hey, it's mine. I said I'd share, not play take away."

She put the notebook on the table between them and started at page one.

Fred couldn't help explaining the basics to her even though she was the true science nerd, "It's your basic black lab notebook. See he dates it, and if it looks like something is important, he gets someone to sign and witness. Just like my school lab book. Except this one was for real. And this one says TOP SECRET across the top of each page."

Rhonda nodded, not listening, as she turned the pages. Most pages were filled with equations and drawings. Rhonda looked closely and understood a bit. Fred understood nothing.

"This is not your bonehead math. Way over my head," Fred pointed out. "Let's look for pretty pictures, that's my level."

Rhonda read, "And thus, the direction can be reversed in small fields!!!"

"The t in that equation, is that time?" asked Fred. "I only do real stuff like transistors and tubes—we don't use equations much. I leave the heavy math to big thinkers like you. So, help me. Is the t time? Is that what they're reversing?"

Rhonda spoke slowly and nodded her head. "What are those mad scientists doing? A little time machine?" Of course, she didn't believe it could be a time machine but wanted to know what was in this notebook that someone had braved an explosion to grab. The time machine idea would keep Fred's sci-fi movie mind going as he stared at its incomprehensible pages, and, hopefully, he would not throw it away until she had checked it.

"I want to show this to my friend Nunzio, OK?"

"Wait, it's going into trash. Or maybe I'll burn it."

"Our government that already can blow up the whole world may now be fooling with time. Do you want time to start acting funny? You want to be ninety years old tomorrow or go back to being a snotty, five-year-old kid? Now go get a shower and smell like a human before we go to bed. I'm going to keep working on the notebook until you get dry."

MONDAY

Monday Morning

Fred pulled on his jeans and plodded into the kitchen, bare-chested, bare-footed, and fuzzy headed from sleep. He pulled out a bag of granola from the cabinet and filled a bowl that had been sitting in the drainer.

"See any milk?" he asked and got a head shake from Rhonda who was finishing a cup of black coffee, so he ran cold water into the bowl.

"Want breakfast?"

Rhonda looked at the half-drowned cereal swimming in tap water and declined. She was ready for the day with only coffee, ready for one of her city walks—no work for her that day. She was a part-time wait-drudge Friday through Sunday and a reader and walker on her days off.

Fred was ready, too, maybe for another hour of sleep or maybe for a look at his electrical circuits text. The lab class on campus didn't start until three.

"So, who's Nunzio?"

"He's a grad student. He might know what the notebook means."

"Enough people know about it already—two is more than enough; three isn't just a crowd, it's a conspiracy."

"Actually, two is a conspiracy as far as the law goes, and anyway, Nunzio's cool and can keep quiet. He's from Sicily where they cut your parts off if you talk."

"And we're from America where they lock you away if you read something Top Secret, and then there is the whole bombed building thing. That will keep the FBI on their toes. On our toes, too if we don't watch out."

Fred read aloud from the newspaper:

San Francisco, Ca.—An explosion that police said was caused by a bomb damaged a building on the Livermore Lab grounds injuring two staff members. One person is missing. A group calling themselves the Summer Soldiers has claimed responsibility.

"I bet I'm the missing person." Fred pointed at himself.

"You're never quite all there but a missing person—that's overstating the problem."

"You're the one missing half the time." They had this discussion often. Rhonda would disappear on long walks through Golden Gate Park when she wasn't working. She called them resets.

Rhonda passed on Fred's second offer of watered granola and left going down the back kitchen stairs to the yard and through the gate onto Capp Street. She had the notebook buried in her purse.

Fred worked his molars hard on the damp granola and sprayed out a messier than usual verse:

> *Granola makes your teeth all chewy*
> *That's exactly what it do-ey.*
> *I'm caught in big legal jaws*
> *Fate has got me by the balls.*

The front bell rang. Fred pulled the handle at top of the steps releasing the front door catch and yelled, "Come on up. You'd save money, Paul, if you just moved in with Louise. Next time remember the key when you come home."

But it wasn't Paul. The men on the stairs were suits, basic detective grey. Fred was a slow learner about opening the door.

"You Fred Arnold?" Fred nodded. The one on the right waved a badge. "FBI. Want to come with us. And we have a warrant." Two more entered the room and started eyeballing the bookcases and closets.

"Thank God the notebook had gone off for a long walk with Rhonda," was all Fred could think as he was guided into the back seat of an unmarked special.

Fred sat in a bolted-down metal chair behind a bolted-down table in a small room in the big federal building near San Francisco's City Hall. A black, window-darkened, oversized Ford had brought him into an underground garage where his escorts walked him to an elevator that took a key to get into and had no buttons—no floors were marked; no lights flashed as they rose. When it stopped, they walked him shoulder to shoulder down a dim short hallway and finally into the room with the metal table.

He sat and twiddled his thumbs while he waited. He figured some secret window had half the FBI keeping track of his scratching, yawning, and twiddling. He sang to get rid of the jitters:

> *I sit here twiddling away*
> *Waiting for the police to play*
> *A good game of tell me, lad,*
> *Why you evil? why you bad?*

A half hour had passed when the door finally opened, and a tall man came in and sat across from him, leaning forward. A small one stood in the back running a tape recorder.

"I'm Agent McCreedy. Operating the recorder is my assistant. Now tell me what happened, and all will be fine."

McCreedy looked basic East Coast preppy with an FBI overgloss. He clipped his words into a tight toothy punch. Both men were thirty-something buzz cuts with skinny ties that could strangle. McCreedy smiled enough to hurt his teeth. Fred tagged him Agent Sunshine and forced a return smile, spreading his lips out cheek to cheek, and then, looking up from the table, started in, "I was in the Plutonium Room, and it all went crazy."

Fred went through his escape—the doors locking, the hallways, the stairs, the smoke and flames, the window, the roof, the hill, the front gate, the pickup, and finally the fleas. It took a half hour. He said nothing about the ferret-face. It was easy to tell the story minus him and minus the notebook he had picked up and stuffed in the back of his pants when he climbed out the window. He dropped Rhonda and the time machine from his spiel and didn't mentioned Paul or anyone else. It was his story, his and the fleas.

Fred wanted to sing a version of his answers. He knew it was not time for his talent to shine, but his brain kept fighting for airtime, blowing out a mostly silent four lines:

> *Find that notebook, go grab Fred*
> *Lock him up until he's dead.*
> *Don't believe him, it's a lie.*
> *Beat him, make this bad boy die.*

"That was a narrow escape, son." The agent deadpanned as he sat looking straight into Fred's face. Fred looked straight into the table.

After three minutes of the silent treatment, Fred needed to do something. He had nothing more to say and could not sing to this guy unless he wanted the looney bin, so he started talking about how great granola was with nothing but water. That ended the interview.

"The head agent will be here in a few minutes to verify everything you said. Anything else to add before he arrives?"

Sunshine and his partner left after Fred shook his head. Fred looked around. Nothing in the room but an air vent and a door and the table with his elbows sitting in something sticky. He sat waiting for an hour.

> *Sitting with the FBI, spilling all my beans.*
> *They want fry me, fry, fry, fry, by semi- legal means.*
> *Oh Fredrico, don't you cry for me,*
> *You come from Argentina with old Eva on your knee*

The boss agent finally entered the room eyeing Fred. He carried a folder that he dropped on the table. There was no second agent with a recorder, but Fred guessed that the walls had a mic and the recording had already started.

"I am Supervisor Andrews. Think of me as your priest hearing confession.

Andrews looked like an aged version of McCreedy. His flat top had grey, his jowls hung, his eyes bagged. The suit looked upscale and darker, the tie wider. He had the same proper manner as the earlier agents, something only the FBI or Mormons could pull off in the 1970s. He spoke slowly like he was chewing his vowels. He scared Fred.

"You are in trouble son. You need to tell us all."

"I told Mr. Creedy everything.

"Mc-Creedy. Now tell me."

Fred went through the same story. The boss agent stared. Fred dropped his gaze to get away from the eyes.

"Now we have witnesses who saw you with a partner when you were on the roof.

Fred decided to add the ferret-face to his story, noting that he was too far away to see anything but his back. And the notebook was still tucked into the ass-end of his brain where he would never talk about it.

"You know that life could be hell if you don't tell all."

The interview with his high priest confessor ended. Ten minutes later Fred met the next level up in the agent hierarchy. He entered the room chomping a cigar stub. Paul figured him for the heavy of the group. He was dressed for it—wrinkled suit, tie hanging low, belly bulging blimp-like. Maybe fat, maybe old sagging muscle, but it filled him out as he thumped down into the chair and dropped a red folder with Fred's name on it on the table.

"Looks like Agent McBastard to me," was all that Fred could think.

"Why didn't you call us?"

Fred choked on his spit when he tried to talk but finally got out an answer, "I had to work. I was going to call you today. See, I have your phone number right…"

"You didn't think it was important that the United States of America had been attacked? You just slinked away and went about your oh-so-important life while crazed radicals blew up a secret United States Government facility?"

"The Lab is secret? It was wide open having Family Day, and I was going to call you. First thing. Really." Fred held up his napkin with the phone number on it.

"Your friend, your—what shall we call him?—a co-conspirator?—wrote our phone number on a napkin?"

"We don't conspire; we eat together."

"And you discuss—what shall we call it?—propaganda? Like the books in your room?"

"You mean textbooks? I'm in college and have to read them."

"You have Marx and you have that commie Marcuse sitting in your room."

"I have Abe Lincoln in there too."

"So, you two discussed commie books."

"No one calls Abe a commie when I'm around."

"Now, what did you and this so-called FRIEND bring with you to the lab in that little FOREIGN car of his?"

The interview was not going well. Paul and Fred looked like sacrificial hippie lambs on a short walk to the local House of Mutton.

"How long have you known this Paul," he looked down at his notes, "KEN-DIZZ-ER-SKY?

"You pronounce it: KEN-JER-SKI."

"I don't give a damn if it's KEN-JERK-OFF-SKI. How long have you known him?

The interview proceeded farther downhill. It fell off a cliff. Fred tried to answer the truth, but he kept the Lab notebook stashed deep in his cortex and his friends in there too. He soon realized, though, that he was not simply answering questions. He was answering for all the sins of all the hippies of the world. This agent, whatever his name was, did not like long hair, funny clothes, incense, bare feet, mary-juana, names like

Fawn and Starlight, and especially did not like long-hairs getting jobs in an H-bomb factory.

"Let's go over what happened yesterday, and this time tell the WHOLE FUCKING TRUTH! First, why did you go to the lab? You wanted to watch it blow up? Do you know these radicals; these Summer Soldier fuckups?"

Fred went back through his trip from the front gate's welcome sign to the back of the pickup with his travel mates, the fleas, once again during the next hour.

"It was smokcy and I only saw his hair from the back." Fred didn't want to say he had the ferret-faced man's looks locked in his eyeballs. If he had, he would spend the rest of his day looking at mug shots. He'd seen those crime movies with the witnesses getting googly-eyed after hours of photos of our finest evildoers."

"You're in trouble, son. You are deep-shit trouble." Lead Agent McBastard banged the table and then stood and walked out. Fred sat for another hour, wondering what was going to happen, and then something he didn't expect appeared. A woman walked in, asked him his name and escorted him to the door.

Fred waited for the "don't leave town" lecture that always was in movies, but only got was a business card with an FBI shield, a long acronym, and a phone number.

Monday Afternoon

Time had flown. The sun had done its morning's work
and half the afternoon's while he had entertained the FBI. Too
late for his lab class, Fred was late for the whole day, but
definitely late for lunch. His stomach growled an unhealthy roar
and brought him back to his normal, belly-driven reality as he
walked out of the Federal Building. Fred went on the hunt, head
down, stomach out, sniffing for something with meat. Nothing
near the Feds. Anyway, he wanted space between himself and
the FBI. He jaywalked the street and hopscotched the Civic
Center. Normal humans filled its sun-lit plaza: drummers beat
congas alongside their smaller brothers playing bongos;
dancers—barely post-pubescent, in long, thin, homemade
dresses—spun slow, drugged circles, looking up at the sun; older
hippies lay on the grass; dogs spread out with them.

Hippies needed more love than old-style San Francisco
was willing to give—so they all had a puppy or a dog—and the
canine crew always obliged with its style of affection, licking
faces and showering saliva on those they loved. Their masters
rewarded their four-legged charges with beads, bandanas, and
dog chow. Fred walked by and they licked at his legs. Hippie
canines were always on a love fest.

Nothing nearby to eat. Down to Market—a
construction mess of a street. The streetcars were being moved
underground into a big hole, a hundred feet deep, running the
length of the business district. Sidewalks were blocked, shops
folding. Restaurants dead. You couldn't walk because of

barricades. Cheap theaters and, worse for Fred, cheap food joints were gone. He walked five blocks past the barriers to Tops, a diner on life support, but still cranking out high class grease, a diner with a red picket fence and shutters on the outside and red stools inside. He took one and did a Biggie Burger, along with a pile of fries floundering in a reservoir of catsup.

Eight bites later, after the burger was deep in Fred's inner sanctum, and the remaining fries looked on in fear, Fred scanned for flatfoots hanging about. No one inside had a buzz cut. He was sure he was not off the hook with the Feds, hoping to be, but too real to believe in fairy tales. He figured the FBI treated everyone as they had him—a ride downtown, a search and hopefully not-destroy mission in his apartment, followed by a little early affection starting with Agent Sunshine and then Father Confessor Supervisor, all topped with a verbal beating from McBastard. Now would they follow up with a tour de city, putting agents on his tail.

An early edition of the Examiner was in a rack outside, so Fred pulled back a dime of his thirty-cent tip lying on the counter, walked out, and dropped it in the coin box while scanning the headline. "Summer Soldiers Manifesto." He pulled out a paper and read, "We are incensed. We are mad. We are Sunshine Soldiers demanding immediate withdrawal from Vietnam, reduction in the military budget, workers committees on the board of every company, and an end to nuclear arms." Sounded right for a Berkeley manifesto. He read past the details to the final sentence in the article: "The FBI, ATF, and local enforcement agencies have set up a task force headed by the Western Division Sub-Directorate of the FBI."

"The gov isn't holding back. They probably have half the force working on the case. It's time to get in touch with Rhonda to tell her to lay low and drop the notebook unless she wants a date with the FBI and not me tonight."

After telling his last three fries he would never forget them and would only be gone for a minute, he folded the newspaper and scrunched into a payphone booth at the back of the diner, singing as he dialed:

> *Many, many manifestos,*
> *I got mine, the very best-o.*
> *I demand stuff 'cause I care-air.*
> *All the world's wrongs - in my hair-air*
> *and in my face and on my head,*
> *My manifesto says I'm DEAD.*

The phone kept ringing. No answer. "Rhonda must still be in the park. I need her to trash everything connected to my excursion into H-bomb land."

Fred walked in the direction of Golden Gate Park, planning to cut through the Haight. He was a walker, a tall one who could outstride most folks. San Francisco was a walking city—seven miles from tip to tail, two hours max to cross the whole thing for Fred's steps.

> *You can walk anyplace.*
> *You can raise the dust.*
> *You can walk anywhere*
> *quicker than a bus.*

This was Fred's Manifesto.

Before searching for Rhonda, he needed to see if the FBI was following. He saw the standard slew of hippies crowding the streets as he approached the Haight, not domesticated demi-hippies like Fred, but true feral ones that crashed any place at night, picked through free clothing boxes, lined up in the Panhandle for a meal, and dosed on acid and mescaline often enough to make them a basic food group. These young ones were wandering lost like the lilies of the field, like duckies without their mom, like the sheep that skipped out on Bo Peep. All waiting to get sheared by the cops, the pimps, and the hustlers. But changing everything.

Fred wandered through them. No crew cuts in suits were visible, but Fred was sure the FBI had its undercover troops out looking for those Summer Soldiers and probably him too, agents in long-hair, hippie drag. "Hell, I read mysteries. I know something about this stuff." But Fred's undercover reading only covered the basics. He dredged up everything in his brain. He stopped and tied his shoelaces looking back to see who was there, he dropped his keys and bent down looking around, he window shopped and checked out reflections, trying to spot anyone following him.

He only saw hippies when he looked back. He saw them ahead. Hippies here and hippies there, crowding walks and walking the street. They attracted a tour bus crawling down Haight Street. Passengers snapped photos as they would of hippos and hyenas in Africa. Fred smiled at the cameras, but their lenses were looking for more exotic game. The most brazen of the local fauna banged on the bus and gave out a price list: "A dollar for smoking dope, five for something naked."

Safe behind their closed bus windows, couples snapped at hair, flowers, sewn-on patches, beads, scarves, bellbottoms, and bare feet. "Bare feet on filthy streets—yaahh," a high-pitched, middle-aged voice called out from the seat behind the driver. Fred looked down. Dozens of dirty, dark-stained, crusty, smiling bare feet. But as Fred looked, he saw one pair dirty yes, but with clean white ankles and barely scuffed soles, having none of the patina of the city's effluvia that the others had earned. Mr. White Ankles was thirty feet behind Fred in a record store doorway, squatting and looking away, trying too hard to fit in with the natural animal life of the Haight. He wore a buckskin jacket with beaded fringes, a pair of hand-woven pants from south of the border, a well-worn, over-the shoulder sports bag, and a beret. A dress outfit, too clean for afternoon wear. Something a cop might think was basic hippie attire after seeing a photo spread about the Haight in *Life* magazine. And the hair—it must be a wig—clean and shiny, ready for a shampoo photo shoot.

Fred stood, started walking, but turned away from the park and his hunt for Rhonda. He headed up Stanyan Street, making sure to avoid any Rhonda run-in. She had to remain his secret. He looked back. White Ankles was on the move. Right behind him.

Fred headed to UC Hospital near the park where he could lose himself. He had accomplished this on two or three occasions when he visited friends doing time on the third floor. The buildings climbed one of the hills that San Franciscans call mountains, forming a maze of connections and walkways with floors galore, but most important, with many entrances and exits. A great place to cat and mouse a flatfoot tail.

White Ankles had pulled a costume change and was trying to mix with the hospital visitors in front of the main building. He had on clodhopper shoes—but no socks so the ankles still showed—and a Forty-Niners jacket. The beret and wig had disappeared. Now his short hair showed signs of a recent trim, probably for morning inspection. The sports bag bulged, probably holding his recently removed hippie ensemble.

> *Looks like a cop with no mop on his top.*
> *Hair wont flop with his short cop chop*
> *He's got to pay his policeman dues*
> *Wearing those god-awful shoes.*

Fred sang as he loped up the stairs to the hospital's front door. He pushed into the main entrance and grabbed an elevator already packed and heading up. One floor and then out and down the hall into a waiting room—OB Gyn. He didn't fit in with the twenty pregnant women sitting there, so he turned for the gents', slid in, and grabbed a stall. Cleanest he had ever seen. Probably his visit was its first that day—not many male folks going this way. He filed that into his brain and sat feeling safe. After 15 minutes, betting his tail was at loose ends looking for him, he poked his head out into the hall and followed a twisted path through one building and on to the next and the next.

Thank God for goofy architecture
Hospital halls and rooms for lectures
Buildings huddled for the masses
I'm heading where they give you glasses

Three hallway twists, two turns, and a stairwell later, Fred found Ophthalmology. He knew it because Paul and his myopic, weirdly shaped eyeballs needed an escort home after the docs did the drops and prescribed even thicker lenses. Fred had explored the place when waiting for his housemate to get examined and knew the department had a back door facing the land where nurses roamed, forbidden to males, but he would hop fences and lose his tail ducking back there. Then off to the races, both feet forward into the park, and hopefully a Rhonda rendezvous.

Fred thought of the places he had wandered on his roam-abouts in the park—not really searches for Rhonda but walks where he wouldn't mind a bump into her. He was not a stalker—well, maybe he was, but not a good one.

My heart will never ever flounder.
It's a fish that likes to wander.
'fraid of washing up on shores
and thrashing there forevermores.

Golden Gate Park began about halfway across the city from the bay and then slid down a gentle grade for three plus miles, all the way to the ocean. It started out well organized with museums and playgrounds, league ballfields, and a bandshell, and got wilder with woods and lakes and finally big fields where organized rock concerts happened about once a month. Unorganized ones featuring drums and maybe a flute or sax happened somewhere every day.

Fog ruled the park during the summer except during early afternoons in its eastern extremes. It was a place for keeping warm by walking, running, or roller skating, a place for action—not for lolling in the sun in your skivvies, as some did anyway on Hippie Hill where no one noticed the cold. They barely noticed anything as they danced and sang away.

"Now what would Rhonda do?" Fred tried thinking Rhonda style. "She's a flowery kind of woman. A plant person." Fred wondered why he hadn't thought of looking in the gardens before. His earlier searches had been in places he liked: the lake with rowboats or the smaller lakes with model boat races, the windmill, the cafeterias in the museums, and the soccer and baseball fields to watch games.

He stopped first at the glass-and-wood copy of the Brit Victorian Conservatory and checked out its warm, humid hall smelling more like an English snake farm than San Francisco—but no Rhonda. Then off to the Shakespeare Garden traipsing through its transplanted tulips and rosebuds—nope. Finally, the Arboretum. The name sounded like a home for wayward trees, but flowers lived there too.

Fred walked past the gift shop, through the entrance grounds, and looked first in the fuchsias. No one but plants. Then with Fred turning out onto the lawn, on the grass in one of the few rays of sunshine peeking through fog lay Rhonda eyes closed, doing her mental reset.

> *Rhonda, Rhonda in the grass*
> *Lying, letting her life pass.*
> *Next to trees and barky bowls*
> *Furry squirrels in nutsy holes*

Rhonda jumped, opened her eyes, and saw Fred kneeling beside her.

"I told you this is *Me* time. *Me.* Did you follow me here?"

"I used my deductive powers to find you and we need some *WE* time because of our *WE* problem, The Notebook. Uncle Sam nabbed me and thinks I'm one of those radical lab bombers."

"Bomber? You're a marshmallow not a firebrand. They must have figured that out by now."

"They roasted and toasted me all morning in their interrogation room."

Fred explained Agent Sunshine and McBastard, and the tail to the hospital and his back-door escape.

"What do you want me to do? Turn myself in?"

"I just want us to get rid of that damned notebook."

"Nunzio still has it, checking to see how hard they are screwing our universe."

"Well, get word to him to dump it. And I don't want to know him—I don't want any trail from him to me, and we need to figure out how to keep you out of this.

"That's easy. You take a walk, and I won't. I'll go back to my Rhonda time. You do some Fred time somewhere else and call me in a day or two. Not from your phone—who knows what the Feds will be doing to you by then. And don't worry about the notebook. I'll take care of it. And be careful. You're not that bad a guy and I'd hate to see you locked up because you had to go visit the bomb lab when I told you to stay home."

She touched his hand and then rolled over. Fred stood. He had hoped they would make a great team to get him out of trouble.

> *Like Hera and her big man Zeus,*
> *like Rocky and his dimwit moose*
> *like Nora, yes, and her man Nick*
> *Fred and Rhonda'd do the trick.*

But team time had been canceled. He was on his own and, anyway, it was better to keep her safe and far away. He walked out the Arboretum gate and there in the gift shop looking closely at a book on growing flowers stood Agent White Ankles.

Monday Late Afternoon

"You left her just like you did me after the bomb blew. I sense a pattern in your behavior. And not a good one."

"I didn't want to lead the tail to Rhonda. I didn't want him to see her."

"Like he hadn't seen her already. She's dead meat after your little Judas run. Then you come over here to my place to plant a big wet one on me while looking innocent like Bo Peep dangling her tail behind her."

"But the FBI knows you already."

"Way too well." Paul looked down at the official letter on the kitchen table. He handed it to Fred. "They put me on leave—not exactly fired, but not paid. Put me out to my living room pasture. I thought it was because of your escapades, but all new employees with provisional clearances are sitting home right now."

"What clearance?

"They weren't too strict about it last week unless you were working on war shit in the lab, but now after the explosion yesterday, it looks like everyone's jumpy, and I might need a Top Secret just to get through the gate."

"Top Secret? I thought you were saving the world. Is that a secret?"

"No, but my work neighbors build bombs. You think they are going to let anyone get in after that explosion? They're acting like someone stole the formula for the Big One?"

"Bomb formulas?"

"They'll interview everyone I ever knew before I get my clearance—my old army commander, scout master, ex-girlfriends, and even you—especially if you're not in jail. Thank God, I'm clean. I'm only a dope-smoking, anarchist, ex-army-machine gunner, and mortar dropper. The worst is I've got to tell Louise when she gets in. Together time is what I'll call it. No more commute, no more work, no nothing. Only conjugal bliss with the piquant zing of starvation as we sit in her rent-due apartment."

Fred had found Paul, not at home but at his girlfriend Louise's. She shared it with two other women in a three-bedroom cut out of a Victorian in Bernal Heights, a place well off the beaten track for new arrivals to the city, out past the big Sears on Mission in a neighborhood where the old-time families raised kids and grandkids and worried about these new long-haired settlers. The attractions of the area were many: cheap rents, available apartments, a big Safeway down the hill, and jitney service to downtown. For $260 a month Louise and her roomies—including Paul as a three-nights a week boyfriend—had big rooms and a bath with a real tub for her and a toilet that needed fixing for Paul to work on, a back yard that Paul and Louise had talked into growing veggies, and an impossibly crowded street to park on if you had a car. But who had a car in the city?

Fred had bused over—he broke his walk-everywhere-mandate thinking not of time saved, but of a seat to rest his legs after covering half the city that day—riding on the No. 19, lumbering out Mission Street, past the Chat and Chew and

Donut Heaven, places where life had seemed simpler the day before. Fred looked out the window, not looking for his FBI following, just knowing it was there. They already knew Paul, had his fingerprints from the lab, and probably were checking at that minute to see if he was a bad guy. Or if he was someone Uncle Sam could trust. Of course, in those days our national Uncle couldn't trust anyone under thirty. And vice versa.

"Well, there's another thing I ought to tell you. I took something when I was running out of the building. But the other guy—the one who had the safe open—he took more. I just picked up his droppings." Fred explained the open safe, the ferret-faced man jumping through the window, the briefcase, and the Top Secret notebook.

"You screwed me double. What is this, fuck-your-buddy month? What were you thinking? Go turn yourself in right now."

"Well, Rhonda has the notebook, I think. She may have given it to some Italian guy."

"She'll probably get a warrant nailed to her backside to match yours. Probably mine, too. Don't tell me more—I want to know nothing. Just get that book back. And anything else Top Secret and whatever the hell else you can think of."

"I'm glad you're taking this well."

"I'm cheery because I'm going to kill you if I don't get my job back."

Girlfriend Louise arrived, hugged Paul, and looked warily at Fred. She had a what-are-they-up-to look in her eyes. Then Paul showed her the letter and the yelling started.

"That big slob friend of yours got you booted out? I should boot you out."

Sitting quiet in the parlor
Better than the bath or hall or
in the bedroom with that couple
trading screams; it ain't their nup-tials

Fred slunk out the door.

TUESDAY

Tuesday Morning

The Incense Factory was cranking. Seven packers sat around the big table where they kept counting out a dozen sticks and tucking each dozen into a cardboard sleeve. They would do this all day and sometimes all night when their rent was coming near. Three cents a sleeve added up if you worked twenty-four hours a day.

"It's like meditation. You sit and do. Your mind is free. Freedom at three cents a pack." Daniel, the owner of the Incense Factory, often combined his spiritual beliefs with low pay.

Today the packers laughed and sang along with the radio. It wasn't the Dead or Quicksilver, but the munchkins blasting, "Ding, dong, the witch is dead…"

"What's happening?" Fred called out as he walked in.

"You never know do you? Life is happening. You only

have to tune in." Frankie the resident acidhead often listened in to the heavens as he counted sticks. He was the most tuned in worker in the place.

"J. Edgar died last night," Down-to-earth Linda-Lou filled in the facts. "I wonder what his boy Clyde will do now that the Number 1 G-man, the FBI's fat boy and dress up doll, is going undercover, six fucking feet undercover?"

Everyone had talked about Hoover, the head of the FBI, living for years with his man Clyde as two confirmed bachelors. Linda liked to garnish the stories with Hoover's famed crossdressing tendencies.

"KSAN has been celebrating, playing the same song for two hours. Rumpled Foreskin is our man," Frankie added. KSAN, San Francisco's tuned-in. turned-on station, ruled the airwaves as its announcers liked to say and Rumpled was the Bay's DJ of the hour.

Larry with the Jewish afro danced with pony-tailed Ben in an exaggerated doh-si-doh. Marjorie Eveningstar kept her head down, banging the rivet machine that locked each pack's fold-over top and sometimes a fingernail if the packer was meditating too hard. On J. Edgar Day, she stayed in the here-and-now, keeping time with the dead-witch chorus.

"I bet the FBI will be busy."

"Yes, they're calling in agents for the funeral. We ought to go, too."

Fred was thinking of a different direction as he walked into the dipping room and stared at the frangipani and watermelon barrels. Their stocks were low, but Fred was not here to make incense, he only wanted a place to think, but a song had to come out first.

> *J. Edgar dropped his evening gown.*
> *Clyde, he felt he'd been let down.*
> *J. Edgar slid down in his grave.*
> *Never even gave a wave.*

"I did nothing wrong, if you don't count the notebook, so the key is getting rid of it and Rhonda said it would be done, so I'm fine. I am fine. I'm fine."

"You take up chanting?"

Daniel stuck his head in. He guided the business and the gang of long hairs, mystics, guru followers, and granny-glassed women who made their living from the ungodly smells in the old warehouse.

"I got a call today from our blue-uniformed friends. They asked about you. I gave you a sterling recommendation. What happened to you?"

"I was there when the lab blew on family day, day before yesterday, with my friend. And I ran when the alarms went off and now, they're checking me out."

"Never run, always walk slowly toward the exits—the first rule in movie theaters and in life. But in the heat of action, one sometimes forgets. I know." Daniel had done time on a tax rap a few years back. Fred assumed that was when he had run.

Daniel came near and gave Fred a squeeze around his shoulders. "With all this going on, you should stay away for a couple of days. Let's say a week. I can get Ben to make incense.

I'd rather the cops didn't nose around. And please, call me before you come back. On the special number. And don't use names."

The special number was his lawyer's. No one was too sure about all the things Daniel imported. It was best not to know.

"But we need frangipani."

"Don't worry. Frangipani can take care of itself. Take the old VW van and head north. Maybe to Ma's ashram or the river commune."

"But…"

"Here's the keys. Now go. And good luck"

Tuesday Noon

"Paul, grab my sleeping bag and a change of my underwear and meet me at the Chew. Watch out for a tail. The FBI is on the loose, probably following you and me."

"Didn't you hear they're busy? J. Edgar…"

"I know but, in their alphabet, bombing comes before burial, so watch out."

"I'll use the back door out of the house."

Fred sat in the Chew, working his way through a pile of fries. Fred used the Chew to still his mind when he had problems. Some meditate to find peace; but others eat to be fulfilled. Fred was a latter-day eater and a believer in the holy hamburger and its blessed mother, Sister Mary Lambchop. He believed in whatever worked its way into his digestive system. A guru psychologist led him on his high caloric path to enlightenment in his best-selling handbook, *I'm OK, You're OK*. Fred's *OK* was soaked in catsup. And what could be better with catsup than a double order of fries. Maybe a triple.

Fred chewed over his plan. It was simple: RUN. When the FBI's after you, to hell with Daniel's ideas about walking slowly toward the exits. A tank full of gas and stomach full of fries could power him beyond the government's grasp. The highway was his path to enlightenment, and it's true that maybe his path led nowhere, and his van, after hauling incense for ten years, gave out fumes like some hippie heaven or more likely a hippie hell, but with the windows down and Fred's nonfunctioning nose, he was as happy as any most-wanted FBI poster boy could be.

As the last fries went down, Paul walked in.

"I'm ready. Where're we heading?"

"What do you think this is, a road trip buddy flick?"

"I have no job, my woman threw me out, the pigs are following my footsteps, and you need help. You've always needed help. Remember I saved you when the cops climbed the stairs, and the box of stems and seeds was on the table…"

"Tell that story one more time, and you're going to take flying lessons out the front window."

Fred started a staring contest. Paul cut it off.

Tuesday Afternoon

Paul started singing:

> *I want to be free*
> *Like a big hippie tree.*
> *Driving, driving driving my truck*
> *In an octapus's garden mucky muck muck...*

"Come on, Paul. You're bad and stealing from Ringo and anyway I'm the singer in the group. You're the silent, sullen sidekick. And you have nothing singable in your head even with a joint stuck in it."

Paul had slipped into his old smoking ways after losing his girl and his job.

"I can sing anything," Paul said. "You're stuck on grade-school rhymes and adolescent dreams. I'm singing in the classic pickup truck genre."

Fred opened the window and blasted his vocal cords at full volume:

> *Heading up the byway*
> *Not some concrete flyway.*
> *Never lettin' them see,*
> *I'm high, I fly, I'm me*

"That's a freedom song for you."

Paul hadn't talked Fred into letting him come along. He'd started yelling for the FBI in the Chew. And followed Fred when he ran out the door. Paul was not above vocal blackmail for a seat in the van.

He had his bare feet on the dash riding shotgun while Fred continued his singing duties:

> *Hippies, hippies left and right,*
> *Seen the aura, seen the light,*
> *Chanting to a different drum*
> *Hippie gurus, hippie scum.*

He wove the steering wheel back and forth in four-four time as they drove up Route 1 along the coast. After four hours of rocks, beauty, surf, and bad brakes, he turned inland heading toward a commune near Philo, an old logging and sawmill town famous for having more people than thumbs. Redneck loggers showed off their stumps in town bars as they got ready for work. They didn't know what to make of the new long-haired arrivals at the commune, but that didn't stop them from buying hippie pot along with their normal six-packs.

Fred followed a dirt road that turned off the two-lane blacktop. Sundown was closing in as Fred bounced the van over ruts and rocks for the final half mile, going past shadows of tall conifers on the unmarked lane lined with poison oak and scrub. The road finally looped in front of an old Victorian that a tree baron had left to his children. After two generations it had fallen to a single heir, a long-haired moneybag—Bigbucks Bartley he was called on the commune—who had succumbed to the joys of acid, music, and a dropped-out life among the hills, rills, and the frills of the hippie ladies. He let the trees grow in peace. He let anyone who could flash a peace sign stay on the land. He let an ad-hoc council rule the place, as long as they left him alone. Council Rule One was work (unless you were Bigbucks) either on the farm growing something edible or smokable or if you were a newbie, packing incense. The council had a verbal handshake with Daniel and the Incense Factory. They would pick up a truckload of incense sticks every week or so and return it bagged and boxed. The Council got the three cents a pack and the packers got food, a bed, music, and often something to smoke.

Incense packing went from noon to nightfall on the Victorian's front porch where the workers consumed more smokables than food. Often a too-relaxed eye shoved more than a dozen joss sticks into a pack, sometimes watermelon or cherry ended up with new patchouli friends, and sometimes the front porch gang just burned incense and stared at its glow, but the council kept them on duty, sometimes leading them in chanting and sometimes having speed-loading contests, but always packing until the overload of porch people had enough and yelled uncle. Most headed back to the city. But they were always replaced with new drop-ins. The best of them asked to work the fields and exercise their nascent farmer muscles growing food. Growing the smokables was the domain of the old timers who disappeared for days when they worked the plants.

Fred pulled the van up to a small cottage behind the Victorian. He honked and Bartley came out sporting his basic rich hippie look: a string of beads, a clean belly button, and loose, low-cut cloth pants handsewn out of Indian bedspreads direct from Cost Plus.

"Welcome to Wanowona."

Bartley had made up the name. He often told the story of how a wolf whispered it into his ear after he downed a pink tab out in the woods. Fred was sure wolves could not pronounce w's but he humored the owner of the place and gave him a peace sign. He introed Paul and climbed out of the van carrying a bag of food and drinks.

"Oh, great leader of the clan, we come in peace."

Bartley liked to be play Native American chief.

"Welcome to my land."

"We'll take a load of incense back to the city but not for a couple of days. My friend Paul and I need to chill out. Daniel told us to just cool it in his cabin."

Fred started down the trail behind the cottage, as Bartley called out.

"Far out, but someone's there. Linda's grandfather. He needed a place to crash."

"But…but…it's ours."

It worked out. Fred, Paul, and Linda's grandpa would live together in the cabin. Cabin was far-too-grand a word for the log lean-to that Daniel had built for his mescaline-fueled vision quests. On one side, an antique window let in the forest shadows and on the other, a leaded-glass door looked amused that it had come down so far in the world after living in a Pacific Heights mansion for a hundred years. The lean-to had its own outdoor john only twenty yards away—a joy because most of the communards shared what they called the world's biggest shitter, an eight-holer, located a fair walk away when nature rang your bell. Residents lived in rooms in the Victorian or in tents or in rough cabins like Daniel's. Electricity was scarce. Lantern batteries and candles lit the night. Amusements were all analog, human, and non-virtual. Most regulars plunked at guitars. One strummed an autoharp. Singing was encouraged along with reading. *The Hobbit, Mao's Little Red Book,* and *Steppenwolf* made the rounds. About forty people composed the current population, roughly split between men, women, and babies, all under thirty, white as indoor ghosts, and living on food stamps, Safeway dumpsters, and Goodwill's freebie bins rather than the still barely productive communal food gardens. The residents had dreams of picking fresh tomatoes and potatoes, gathering eggs, and even milking a cow, but no one knew farming. A few had worked up calluses in the fields, but most preferred a late start and early finish to their workdays. The plants kept asking for more help and dropping dead to show their displeasure.

"Who gets bottom bunk?" Paul was an organizer. He wanted order and predictability in his sleeping life.

"I can't climb with my back acting up, boys. I need the bottom." Grandpa rubbed his kidneys and kneaded his back as he sat on the lower bunk. He was not going anywhere.

"OK, who gets the floor?" Paul went on, looking at Fred.

"I'll take the van. There's foam in the back. You take the top bunk. Enjoy yourself. Now let's eat."

Fred pulled a can of tamales and a pack of hot dogs from the food bag and dumped them together in a pot on the kerosene stove in the cooking area in front of the cabin. Paul pulled out his church key and popped open three beers.

"You eat yet, Gramps?" Fred was trying to figure out what to call the old man sitting in a rocking chair under a tarp stretched in front of the cabin's door.

"I've got a name. Red. It's worked for eighty years. I'm still me, not some old growth of a grandpa that Linda dropped on the place. So don't call me grandpa. And I ate, but I can eat twice."

Red did have red hair once, but it had faded and gotten sparse. His face was red, the sun had worked on him for most of his eighty years. His nose was thin, his lips too. His voice was coated in a southern drawl that made him mostly intelligible. He smiled through his dentures at the food when it was ready— "Mexican-style tamales" (that's what the can said) with a side hot dog slapped on a paper plate. Red held onto his beer and smiled at his plug of tobacco lying on the table, ready for an after-dinner chaw.

Paul and Fred did fast work clearing their plates. Two tamales, three dogs, and a big squirt of catsup each.

"What do you call this haut cuisine of yours, Fred? Maybe next time I'll pick the food, if you don't mind."

"It's not very haut—you just had my gringo dogs and their Mexican friends. I know they live low on your connoisseur food chain, but I was in a hurry. They come direct from fast Fred's school of cooking and fill you with assorted pig parts, cornmeal, and gas. Perfect for life in the woods."

Red chewed slower than the boys, his false teeth were loose and not used to sawing through cheap hot dog skin. He sat straight in his oversized bib overalls. They had fit him five years earlier when he still worked the fields back in North Carolina but now they sagged. Everything on Red sagged. His neck looked like an overworked turkey wattle, his ears dangled in folds and wrinkles, and the skin on his arms drooped. His muscles had shrunk after he quit field work, and his skin had nothing left to hold onto. It hung like laundry left on the line too long.

Gramps relied on his granddaughter to support him. She brought him west to the commune where he was doing fine, rocking, whittling whistles and walking sticks, spitting tobacco, and breathing in the forest.

"You boys goin' to start farmin'?" he cackled. "Farmin' funny weed? I farmed tobacco weed but don't know much about your brand."

"We're only here for a couple of days. But we can work. Right, Fred?"

Fred dropped an evil eye on Paul. Fred was here to lie low, not work. Lying low meant sleeping late. And airing out the incense from his soul. And the FBI from his brain. He needed to wait here until the FBI caught whoever had stolen the books and papers. Then he would reappear in the city. All would be good again.

Fred popped another beer. Red shook his head when offered one. Paul rolled a joint and nodded toward Red. He cackled again.

"I got my weed here." He took a chaw of the tobacco plug.

"Granddaddy, you chewing that nasty stuff again?" a young woman called out as she approached.

"Be good boys, it's my granddaughter. She lives on the warpath."

"You're chewing it again. You know what I told you."

Fred moved into the shadows. He didn't want Linda to see him.

"Who've you got with you?"

"Linda, baby, you got to let an old man be. Now you go back with that skinny butt of a young man, and I'll spit it out. I promise."

"You better."

Linda headed back toward the Victorian.

"She is some woman. Reminds me of my best dead wife. She's trying to get me to teach them how to farm in this place. But I farm tobacco and that's it. They want tomatoes and mary-juana and the like. I don't farm tomatoes. You boys farm tomatoes?"

Fred walked back into the light and took the joint.

"You two look like city boys coming to get a piece of country. Everyone comes to the country these days. In my days, everyone left. My brother Robert, he took a factory job making chairs, and soon after, my sister Loretta, she married some insurance salesman, and before long I was the only one on the farm and they all wanted me to sell it to Mr. R.J. and his friend Reynolds." Red paused. "That's a joke, boys."

Fred took a toke and passed to Paul. Red's continuing chatter became part of the night noises. Crickets, frogs, and as, Red would say, God knows what all. Fred and Paul sure didn't. They knew trains, delivery trucks and sometimes sirens back in the city. They sat back immersed in their dope and the woodsy sounds.

Red looked up at the stars and said, "OK, boys, it's time and it's Friday night. You want to come along to see some real goings on, out here in the country."

Red stood up from his chair, grabbed a hand-carved walking stick as tall as he was, and started into the woods.

"Watch for the snakes, boys." Another cackle.

Fred and Paul looked at each other and did a why not. Fred picked up the rest of the six pack and followed with only a little moonlight and the pinpoint glow of Paul pulling on the joint to guide him. Gramps knew the trail and was far ahead in the trees. The two young men stumbled behind. Fred sang into the night:

> *We are climbing grandpop's ladder—I mean mountain,*
> *getting high, Lord, getting high.*
> *We are rhyming, never doubting,*
> *getting high, Lord, getting high, …*

The three climbed half an hour until they reached a meadow where a long log bench stood next to a spindly table. On the table a small TV, probably the only one in the commune, sat with its screen reflecting the moonlight.

"Showtime, boys."

Red walked behind the TV table, bent down, and yanked a pull cord on a generator sitting on the ground.

"Fifty-four decibels. No one in camp can hear this baby. I got me a kilowatt, more than the rest of the camp altogether. It's time for the Friday Night Fights."

The Gillette shaving jingle sang out, "Look sharp, Feel Sharp, Be Sharp…"

Red settled in and spit a wad of tobacco juice into a can under the TV making it ring, sounding like the bell for Round One. Fred and Paul sat beside him on the bench and watched as Carmine Basilio beat on Chuck Davey. Then Davey jabbed Basilio until he stepped back. Red locked into the screen and was quiet. The boys shook their heads and popped another beer.

The fight went ten rounds. Blood barely showed in the little black and white picture. Basilio staggered Davey, but Davey peppered him with sharp lefts. It looked even.

"Well, that's it." Red turned the channel.

"Don't you care who won?"

"I know who won. Who cares what the damn fools in bowties think, and now I've got to watch the weather. You boys have crazy damn weather in California. Back in Carolina I could sniff and tell you everything—this time of year it was hot and humid, or it rained. That was it. Here it never rains in the summer and the air is as dry as my bones unless the fog comes in."

"How can you get a station here out in the woods. Nothing comes in this far from the city."

"Some smart-ass boys a couple farms over set up a TV station, a clan-des-tine one. With old movies but on Friday, old fights.

"Old fights?"

"Yep, I listened to this one on the radio in my barn back when I had a 160 acres. Chuck Davey fought Basilio in 1952. I always wanted to see that lefty jab. These TV boys a couple miles over are doing a great service to this here country."

"But you get the weather, too. That's not from the past."

"They got some kind of setup to pass on a San Francisco station. They play Oswald the Rabbit during the day for the kids. I used to see him at the movie palace on Saturdays when I was a youngster."

"High tomorrow, sixty at the coast and one hundred inland. Heavy fog in the morning. Now back to Van with the latest on the bombing."

"Well, look at that, boys."

Fred's picture, his senior class picture, doctored with a beard and bushed out hair smiled out of the little screen.

"Fred Arnold, a resident of San Francisco, is sought for questioning as a person of interest…"

"Shit. Shit. Shit and a half," Fred banged on the bench.

"Triple shit." Paul joined in.

"They got a good likeness of you, and you are in definite shit, you got that right." Red added. "Like I was in back after we got them revenuers after us in '49. At the still up in the hills back when brother Robert sold moonshine to farmers when he drove around selling those kitchen trinkets for the ladies and jug refills to the men.

Fred and Paul looked at each other. Red was excited and ran on, "Yep, it was the Jewel Tea Company that sold strainers and pots and towels to the ladyfolk and underneath the delivery truck Robert welded a fifty-gallon tank. I made the corn liquor and Robert sold it. Then the revenuers came up in the hill country looking for us and they got a load of buckshot their way…"

Fred interrupted Red's story, "I really need to lie low starting now. I don't think anyone but Bartley saw me, so we are good out here in the woods."

"Well, I seen you, but don't you worry I don't like them FBIs."

Fred made a full-toothed smile at Red. "Well thanks a million for not turning me in. It'll get you points when you get to heaven."

Fred thought for a minute and said, "Paul, you can show your face, but I'll stay hidden in the lean to."

"Now boys, that's one dumb-assed idea. The fuzz or is it the pigs, I forget what you call 'em these days, they got in-fil-traitors in this place—I can feel it—looking for that loco weed and they will spot you quicker than a dog can drop a turd. I'm going to help you with some advice. You sit right there on your citified asses and pay attention."

Red spit another mouthful of tobacco juice under the TV and started explaining. Paul and Fred nodded. They liked the plan. Red would start work on it in the morning.

WEDNESDAY

Wednesday Morning

Fog blanketed the hills and a fine drizzle fell on the van, its windows covered with long runs of water that made the view from inside into an abstract of forest greens. Fred looked out after pulling on a pair of jeans and a shirt but not finding his shoes. He pushed open the van's side door and headed for the Daniel's private john. The path was wet, cold, and slippery on his bare feet making his bladder's urging even worse, but the door to the outhouse was pulled shut and locked. Fred banged on it.

"Hold on, young man. I was first. First wins in love and possession of the shitter."

As a city kid, Fred wasn't sure of the country rules about peeing in the woods rather than in the john, but he decided adding to the general morning wetness would be unnoticed. After a long splashdown, he zipped up as Red came out of the outhouse door.

Red stretched and proclaimed, "Morning don't start 'til you've had a good shit."

"I take it that your day has commenced." Fred said.

The cool mountain air was contaminated by waves of stink coming out of the john. A country commode is nothing more than a hole in the ground with a seat built over it. It has no flush. When everything piles up, the outhouse, a small shed with a wooden bench, gets picked up and moved to sit over the next hole down the trail. The old hole is covered with a mound of dirt. And a warning sign for anyone who might be thinking about digging.

"Yep, all done. And it's time to get working on you. You know what we decided. Take off your shirt."

"It's cold."

Red paid no attention to Fred's complaint. He reached into an old leather bag. "I've got my granddaddy's bag here. He pulled out something that looked like a pair of pliers for walnuts, or pecans. These here are my grandpappy's pullicans, for pulling teeth—your teeth're OK? I can help if they aren't. But we're here to fix you up. A straight razor—later. And here, this is what we need, hand-powered clippers, good for sheep, dogs, or men. Maybe women too. Squeeze this here handle and your hair gets a snip. Sit and I'll get started before anyone sees you looking like that FBI picture on TV."

Red transformed Fred into Mr. Clean-Cut. The hair on top went; the beard became stubble; the mustache said goodbye. "Now, get a basin and shave that face close. I got the straight razor or a safety Gillette. You can borrow either one," he said waving the straight razor at Fred.

Linda's grandad became Fred's new "Uncle Red" in the plan and Fred wore an extra old suit that Red had packed in case of a wedding or funeral. The suit was short and stopped just below Fred's calves giving him a true country hick look. Both would be wearing baggy suits, wide ties, and white socks—two rubes heading into San Francisco to do the big time, riding down in a Greyhound for a shindig in the city. Fred could do his snooping. Red could enjoy a few days away from his granddaughter and her rules. Paul would drive the van back and take a load of incense to the factory. From then on, they would use payphones to communicate, and Paul would get word to Rhonda. The plan was set.

"I'm taking you out on the town, sonny. The FBI will search those hippie hangouts and never find you because you are now an official Tar Heel tourist. I'll teach you how to dip snuff, whittle a toothpick out of a tree stump, and rock on the porch until it's what you hippies call groovy. That's a joke, son. Groovy. We 'll eat fried chicken and hush puppies and go to movies. We'll live the high life."

Wednesday Afternoon

Fred and Red had copied down the numbers of payphones while Red was doing his whoop-di-do in the big city. They decided to use payphones in the park and listed three of them with times for her to call on the note to Rhonda. They shouldn't wait all day at the same phone booth, so they would have to do their rounds every day.

Fred got the message to Rhonda, leaving an envelope for her at the Owl and Monkey where she worked. It listed numbers and times and, what was for him, a poetic hug:

> *Rhonda, Rhonda, you my gal*
> *Rhonda, Rhonda, you got wow*
> *Call me up and call me quick*
> *We talk happy, make things click.*

In the DeYoung in Golden Gate Park, Fred checked out the paintings; Red gave commentary. "You like paintings, I like suits of armor. Looks like they were midget knights to me."

At three, Fred stood in one of the phonebooths holding a handset to his ear and jabbering to a dead phone while holding the cradle down, waiting for a ring from Rhonda. The only way to hold a phonebooth was to be on a call, and a fake call worked as well as a real one. Nothing rang from Rhonda, so he and Red trouped across the bandshell plaza to be ready for the next time listed on the note, this time for the payphone in the Science Museum. While they waited, they watched kids throwing pennies on Claude the never-moving albino alligator and then did a culinary tour of the aquarium. Red pointed out which exhibits looked tasty and might bite on a good North Carolina nightcrawler.

Waiting here with finny fishes
Dreaming of hamburger dishes
Hoping for a tele call
In the booth right down the hall.

At 4 p.m. in the Science lobby, Fred carried on another fake one-way at the dead payphone while waiting for Rhonda's ring. Nothing rang. At five, he and Red moved on to the next location and sat under the gnarled trees in front of the bandstand listening for a jingle on one of the nearby payphones. Bingo, one went off. Fred ran and grabbed the receiver.

The conversation started with no prelims.

"That was some notebook you gave me. Nunzio took a look. It had data on something called a neutron bomb and now Nunzio won't talk to me. He stuffed the book back in my hands and took off. Looking scared."

"I thought you said he was mafia-bred."

"I said he knew about getting his parts cut off."

Fred had heard about the neutron bomb, an atom bomb that killed all the people but left the buildings and highways unharmed. It was one of those secrets that circulated among the lefties.

"Forget Nunzio and focus on the notebook. We need a good place to burn it. Someplace hot that leaves no remains. Full cremation. Know anyone dead going in for a good toasting? We could slip it in their pocket. That would be best."

Rhonda ignored him.

"Can we meet?" Rhonda asked. "I need to talk to you about your plan to hide out. And I've got to give back this notebook. I don't know where to burn it and I don't want to just trash it. I bet if I threw it in a bin, the whole FBI would play where's the book at the dump until they found it. You're right, death by fire is what it needs."

"Now, more bad news—an agent was there with us at the Arboretum. Somehow he followed me from the hospital."

"I saw him. He took a most fetching pic of me. I had my shirt up over my head, like the mafia dons. He didn't get my face, but he has my bra and ribs on Kodachrome. He ran off when you started sprinting down the path toward the lake.

Red played lookout during the phone call. The museums were closing, and a group of long-hairs exited and came near, tossing a frisbee by the bandstand. He couldn't see the FBI stooping low enough to play frisbee instead of their normal sober-sided cops and robbers games, so he ignored the frisbee flingers and concentrated on the cars driving around the loop between the two museums. He saw nothing but touristy looks at the lion statues and the Tea Garden.

"I know a little restaurant off Clement. Let's meet there at seven." Fred said.

"No hamburgers or dogs."

"No, it's Italian—Giorgio's with the whole nine yards of Romish delights, dripped candles, and just-off-the-boat accents. I'm now the anti-Fred and do more than dogs and burgers. Let the FBI track old Mr. Fred and his bad burger habits. Red and I normally do southern fried, but tonight we'll chow down on pasta with you.

"The new Fred does no rock," Fred continued, "only hillbilly and bluegrass; no outdoor concerts, only old bad movies with Red and his greasy popcorn. And his non-stop commentary. I'm going crazy with his jabber. It'll be great to see you and hear thoughts that are less than eighty years old."

"Maybe you can get him to start blathering in harmony with your songs."

"That was low."

"Remember an anti-Fred sings no ditties. They'd be a giveaway."

He sealed the deal with Rhonda promising to shake any fuzz-tail before her appetizer. She had a plan—get lost in the "Ho, Ho, Ho—Chi Minh, our side is gonna win" peace march on Market Street. Short and small was great for slipping into a crowd. She could duck under all the Fred-sized protesters and be lost forever.

Half the dinner guest list was set.

Fred grabbed a bus and rode while writing a message: "7 PM tonight where we ate after Altman's M*A*S*H." Cryptic enough to be incomprehensible to the FBI but understandable to Paul who had memorably downed two carafes of wine at Giorgio's and did a monumental barf on the bus.

Fred folded the note in half and added on the outside: "Full-sized piano for sale, $3000 - KLondike 6-2459." The secret message was folded inside, the dummy ad on the outside. No one had that many bucks to spare in this neighborhood, so the message would stay up until Paul pulled it down. Or some cleaning committee came by—but this was the Mission, and no one cleaned here.

Fred walked with his notice to the bus stop, a bit too near the Chat and his apartment for comfort, but where Paul had agreed to check every day. A bit of tape and it went on the bus shelter behind the bench.

> *Got a meeting, We'll have chow.*
> *Get that notebook from my gal.*
> *Burn it up to ashes grey,*
> *Hope to live another day.*
> *Or maybe more…*

With that Fred jaunted off to the hotel to listen to Red and his stories until dinner time. Red had gone on a story kick about his agricultural days, about hanging tobacco leaves in a barn to cure, how some heated their barns too hot and smoked the whole crop, and how some burned them down and collected the insurance. Red had days of tobacco stories. Fred had earphones.

Wednesday Night

"It's me. And this is Red. We're from North Carolina visiting. Isn't that right, Red?"

"Yep, this here's my nephew Freddie showing me the big city, and we are out to do the town. Right, Freddie?"

Red and Fred did their down-home act for Rhonda and Paul. Fred in his baggy suit commented on the menu and Red eyeballed the Italian posters on the walls. Paul and Rhonda sat across the table, choking back laughs at the recently shorn farm-boy, the reshod and back-country besuited Fred.

Rhonda had slipped any cop following her in the demonstration, and Paul had gotten the piano sale message and showed up at Giorgio's exactly on time.

"Well, I can't recognize you without your normal mess of a beard and the dirty jeans, but you still have a whiff of patchouli hanging over your head." Rhonda said. "And before I forget it, here's a little present." She handed Fred the black notebook. Fred stuffed it in the back of his suit pants and tucked in his shirt, covering all evidence.

"Yes, you look like a new man, but you still can't come to the apartment looking like that," Paul added. "You're the same age and height and smell as the old Fred. The FBI will make you in a second."

"I could hide out forever looking like this."

"Doing what? You'll need money. You have to work. They'll be waiting. And if you get another job and another apartment, one day you'll slip up on a triple cheeseburger with a donut chaser while the FBI is on duty watching for you and your game is up."

"Your friends are on to something." Red said. "I'm only down in the city for a week, and then you're on your own. That's when our family act is over. I'll have to go back and make sure Linda hasn't gone too hippy on me up there on the commune."

"You can't hide out long enough, Fred. You know that. The FBI won't catch the real bombers. They'll settle for you," Rhonda said as she sucked down a string of pasta. "They're good at catching big city bank robbers, but lab explosions by the kind of people we know, the long hairs, the freaks, they're not the folks that the FBI has on their most-wanted, post office displays. Freaks are new territory for them. We know the hippies just want to have fun while they blow up the world, but the FBI expects greed and sex and money. And worst of all, the FBI knows you and not the real hippie bombers. They'll catch you and you'll end up signing some confession just because you are Fred and then they'll come after Paul and me. We need to figure out what happened at the lab and catch the bombers to get the Feds off our backs. We'll tip off the FBI to end this chase. It's either that or bump off Fred and bury him so deep they never find him."

"I like option A if we have to choose," Fred said as he looked up from his pile of meatballs.

"You're talking about the FBI. I don't collaborate with them. I won't turn in anyone to them. The FBI are the bad guys." Paul stood on his principles as he reached for another chunk of garlic bread.

"Paul, you work for the fucking bomb lab. Of course,

you collaborate." Rhonda raised her voice and noticed the waiter looking their way. She continued in a lower tone. "I have principles too, but I have a life I need to live. I won't do prison well—I'm sure of it. The enemy is still my enemy, but I can give him a hint or two where to look if he'll stop looking for me."

"OK, the lab does bad stuff. I don't work on it, but, you're right—they do bombs. But I have my principles. I do." Paul semi-confessed and semi-whined.

"Theory is good, but how do we find out who did it? We're just bystanders run over by the Feds and the Reds too," Fred was shaking his head. "We're screwed no matter which way the world turns. No matter who's in charge."

"You saw him, the guy with the briefcase. The ferret-face. You're our key. You can identify him" Rhonda smiled at Fred.

"Me, the key?"

Red had kept quiet, looking at his tobacco pouch, thinking it was time for a walk outside to take a chaw. "You boys keep figuring this out and let me know what you decide. Remember I took them Feds on and won back in the '40s. It just takes some fast footwork, a faster car, and a scatter gun. That's what I had." He stood and walked out the door.

"Why is he here?" Rhonda asked.

"He's my cover—you haven't commented much on my new gee-haw look. I'm a southern Mister Clean these days. And most important, he's paying for the food tonight. Been saving his government checks to have a big time in the big city, and he thinks this is it."

"He won't talk, will he?"

"No one would pay attention if he did. He'd mix it in with tobacco growing and corn liquor." Fred said.

There was a pause as Paul and Rhonda looked out the window at Red. Both were shaking their heads as Rhonda looked back at Fred.

"Let's look at what we know. Someone stole something and it included a top-secret notebook that has something bad, bad enough to freak out Nunzio—what did he call it? A N-bomb."

"Who knows exactly what the guy took. We know it was top secret. Bombs are top secret, ergo…" Paul added. He had stopped eating. Even Fred had slowed down. Rhonda had folded her napkin and pushed her plates back a while ago.

Fred spoke quietly, "I heard about it at the vets building on campus." He explained the neutron bomb, the one that kills everyone dead but leaves the buildings intact around the well-cooked bodies. Just what you want if you are taking over. "Great for genocide. The Russians call it the capitalist bomb. It kills the workers and leaves the factories." Fred mumbled out a song:

It was N-bomb genocide.
They bombed my world and then I died.
We were gone, left not a clue.
New people live where I used to

"Does the world know about this neutron bomb?" Paul asked.

"Who pays attention to the type of bomb that kills you." Rhonda said. "You pay attention to the man with the launch button, and then you pay attention to the boom when it goes off. Anyway, the guy who took the plans is probably not going to build a bomb—the big boys on both sides already know how to do that and don't need more plans. Most likely some small-time group from Berkeley wants to publicize what the lab is doing. To embarrass the lab. To embarrass the university that runs the lab. To pull off a full Pentagon Papers on the N-Bomb." Rhonda had become the analyst of the group.

"What if it's some other country?" Paul asked. "Did the ferret-face look foreign?"

"The ferret-faced looked ferret-faced."

"What does ferret-faced mean anyway. He has a snout?".

Rhonda got them back on track. "Let's assume they're Berkeley radicals. If they were foreign, the FBI would be on them—that's what the FBI does. They have all the spies' phones tapped and have more informants than there are spies in the US. But we can take on Berkeley radicals better, quicker, and cleaner than the FBI. We know the territory. We know their habits. We can solve this." Rhonda was excited.

"But wouldn't publishing the plans be a good thing? Letting the world know what's going on here in the Lab? Shouldn't we let them do it?" Fred asked.

Paul piped in, "You want someone building backyard nukes with the plans they read in the Barb? And more important—you want them to do it while you're in jail?"

"I don't want any nukes, so let's find the guys who blew up the lab first and then see what we do." Rhonda looked hard at Paul and Fred. "Who knows any radicals that recently went underground? That's what we're looking for. We need to hit our friends for info."

"That's your plan, Rhonda? Talk to our friends?" Paul asked while rolling his eyes. "How about this—we get the word out that Fred has the notebook." Paul smiled at Fred.

"But they'll come after me."

"You got it, Fred. And you have Red to protect you. And we're here too."

"Red could spit toe-back-ee in their eyes. That's our whole defense, but the bomb guys blow things up. They are not non-violent dudes. I am against violence especially against me. And against you, too, I suppose."

"But they'll come after you and we'll have them." Paul had become excited as the plan evolved.

"Fred, everyone has to make sacrifices. If they get you, we'll always remember you." Rhonda smiled as she spoke. "You'll do it. You know it's the right thing. That's why I hang with you. You may not be the big thinker of the group, but you do what's right."

"But they'll get me. And we are planning to burn the notebook, remember?"

"It makes for juicy bait."

Fred's mind was slipping. He was thinking of bait, himself as bait, and barely noticing the chocolate volcano erupting on the table.

"So how do they find me? Tell me that."

"We give them a phone number. I'll give them mine as the contact and check my phone machine a couple times a day. You two don't have any way to get messages. I've got one of those phone machines that you can play back remotely," Rhonda said.

"But they'll be after you, too. They can do reverse lookups. Even I know how to do that at the city library. I'll be the he-bait and you the she-bait?"

"I'm going underground with you. Got space in that hotel?"

"It's a fleabag."

"Maybe I'll invite you over to my room and share fleas." She winked at Fred.

"What do I do?" Paul asked.

"You're our prime rumor-spreader. You heard Fred found something. Just put the word out. People know Fred and I are semi-items but you two are just roomies. I bet I get a call after they find Fred has something."

"But I'm Fred's roommate. They'll stop by for me before they call you."

"OK, you come and live in the Fleabag Arms with us. It's cheap. Red's cheap so it has to be."

The three nodded at each other.

"OK, next item—how do we stay in touch if we get separated? Rhonda kept the agenda going. "We can't use my message machine all the time. We can't always use pay phones— someone will notice us hanging around them. And we need an emergency system."

Paul made a thoughtful face, "Let's use radio, KSAN. If you're in trouble dedicate a song to mom on the morning show. And make up a name for yourself to let us know where you are, like I'm Turk Masonic or my name is Franklin Van Ness —they don't care about real names on KSAN. And just hang out near the location you give."

They nodded. No one could think of anything better.

Rhonda looked out the window. "Where's Red? But more important, can we depend on him to keep quiet?" She was being practical again.

"Red's on our side, and he's gone a while because chewing tobacco takes time. It's not like a smoke break. You can't spit in here, in a restaurant, like he can in our room."

"OK, we'll move into the hotel late, real late. We want to pack and shake any FBI tails first. I call to adjourn for the night." Paul put on his jacket and Rhonda gave Fred a hug. "Later."

The meal was finished. Fred's mind had slipped from its normal groove when he found he was the bait in this operation. He looked at the happy, spouting chocolate volcano on the table and the dead meatball lying on his plate. It sat silent in the tomato sauce, joyful it was in one piece. Both wondered how they had survived the evening with Fred and his faithful fork and spoon.

The four friends walked together out of the restaurant.

"I'm going to try Louise again."

Louise hadn't spoken to Paul since their blowup after the Family Day lab fiasco.

"Look, tell her I didn't do anything. It wasn't my fault," said Fred.

"It was your fault. You didn't have to go. You didn't have to pick up the notebook. You didn't have to run away."

Rhonda gave Fred a hug as she spoke, "But we still love you. A little at least. Right Paul?"

Paul walked to a pay phone and dialed Louise's number.

"Hello honey girl. It's me."

"Are you with that Fred?"

"Not really."

"Call me when he's dead or out of the country. And when you have your job back."

The call was finished. Paul looked at the receiver hoping for it to say more.

"It's over," he said.

"No, keep trying. She'll take you back. But you let her down. You know that."

"I let her down? I'm the one kicked out—out of work and out of Louise's life. I'm the one going crazy. I need her to understand."

"No one is going to understand why you took Fred to the bomb factory. You destroyed a lot of expectations—yours and Louise's. But you're lucky with us. Friends don't have expectations. Friends don't need to understand. They know you are a screwup and don't care. Now get home and pack up your stuff and we'll meet you at the hotel. It's going to take a miracle to get Fred out of this one. And you and I and this Red guy are going to have to pull him through."

Rhonda finished her say. Fred walked over and hugged Paul.

Red watched and called out, "What's this hugging. You guys are men? Toughen up and let's do it."

"Yea, let's do it," Paul said quietly. "I'll head back and grab some clothes and meet you at the hotel later."

"Don't get followed. Come back late when no one's watching. Real late." Rhonda called to Paul as he walked away. "I'll get a change and see you then. Hold down the fort, Fred. Be good."

She gave Fred a quick hug. The party was over and everyone knew it.

"Come on, son. I'll take you to the movies. That'll put a bit of shine on your day. But I got to give you some wisdom from an old farmer—when things look bad, they probably're going to get worse. That's what farming teaches. That's what life is about. But you gotta keep going and a movie always helps."

Red and Fred hit the movies on Market—a double feature with sticky seats and strange people populating the place, all for a half buck.

"My kind of place after the big prices at the eye-talian eatery," Red said with a smile. "We got us a double feature here with Don Knotts. He is one knee-slapper."

"Who could ask for more than *The Ghost and Mr. Chicken*?" Fred wondered how he got Red duty, but Rhonda had insisted he keep an eye on him.

"*Red Tomahawk*, too. We'll have ourselves a night."

"Red, these movies are ten years old. That's why they only cost fifty cents. They're scratched. They're dirty. The audience doesn't pay for the films; they pay for a place to sleep or do God knows what. This is the cheapest snoozer in town, except the Greyhound station where you buy a twenty-five-cent ticket to San Mateo and go lights out for an hour or two. Here you come in at four in the afternoon and can snooze till they close after midnight with no cops and free popcorn if you don't mind picking it up off the floor—and some of these guys don't mind at all."

"You finished grouching? Want some popcorn? It's clean here at the candy counter and has what the sign calls "almost butter" on it. A shitload of it."

"OK, but first I need to tell you what we three decided in the restaurant while you were out tobacco chewing. We have time before the film starts. Are you up for helping us?"

"Of course. I'm the only one with experience in this group."

"I'm the bait. That will get this fiasco over with. I have something the bombers want, and they'll contact us. We're putting out the word. The bad guys may come after me. And you're near me, in the same room, so they might come after you too. You still in?"

"You got to ask? We're a team. We're almost family. Now let's go in and see movies."

> *Going to watch Red Tomahawk*
> *where Red men die and never balk.*
> *House lights starting to get dim*
> *Hope our ending's not too grim.*

THURSDAY

Thursday Morning

The gang of four assembled for breakfast. Red did a full-American with sausage and eggs, Paul went continental—croissant and espresso, Rhonda took the yoghurt and coffee route, and Fred went full Rice Krispies with a two-banana topper and a coffee side.

"Snap, Crackle, and Pop, you guys. Today is the first day of the rest of your criminal lives. Wake up." Fred poured sugar covering his cereal. "Get your sucrose and caffeine and get on your toes." He emptied his coffee cup and motioned for more.

Rhonda and Paul had moved in after midnight, taking two rooms across the hall. Fred was hoping to room-hop over to Rhonda's, but she put a do not disturb sign on the door and didn't answer any knocks, so Fred did his normal zonked out Zzzzs and woke like a empty-bellied bear when spring hits. He got everyone up at eight banging on their doors and dragged them down to a tiny well-greased diner that that specialized in ursine portions.

"So, you got to sample the Fleabag Arms last night. I warned you."

Rhonda was leaning on the table. She had not slept well on the lumps and scratchy sheets. Paul looked just as tired—he had a room facing the street and listened to sirens all night.

"Great way to start our quest. I'm the bait and I'm the only one moving, except for Red and he's a bystander. Come on, give me some help. You're supposed to keep me from freaking out and thinking about getting done in by the bombers."

Red took a break from chewing on his sausage and said, "Let 'em sleep. They're young and need their growing time."

Rhonda looked straight at Fred and started mouthing words, "Last night lying awake in that room counting the bug spots on the ceiling, I realized we need to plant some big seeds. Not just rely on Paul to spread the word. We need to hurry the message to the bombers. I've been thinking about who might know someone who might know someone else who knows the bombers. I came up with two groups: the Maoists and the Trots. We get them excited. We show them the book."

Paul looked up and added, "How about the vets. Some shaky hangers on show up in the shack at City College."

"You and I hang out at that shack, Paul."

"But it would be a good place to drop a seed and see what grows, right?"

Red kept on chewing, his false teeth fighting the sausage skin. "This here sausage is harder than my arteries."

"You don't have heart trouble. Do you?"

"Well, if I did, it would make a better sausage than this stuff. Who picked this place anyway?"

"We needed something in a hurry. I was hungry," Fred said. "And something close, where we're not out parading ourselves around in front of the cops."

Fred wanted to get his days as bait finished. "OK, let's get ready and start seeding."

"Seeing how you have a gang of two to go with you, I'll head up to that North Beach of yours. I hear they have some tittie shows—pardon my language m'am—But just walking down the street you can see more than in the whole state of North Carolina."

"Go on, Red. Enjoy yourself. We three can handle it,

Thursday Noonish

The 23 Monterey was winding through neighborhood after neighborhood, acting like the bus was lost, going past rich and middle and poor blocks, picking up more and more students heading toward City College. The route seemed designed for maximum tossing from side to side, twisting through minor throughfares that wound themselves along the city's hillsides. Commuting passengers knew the curves and turns, but Fred, stuck between Paul and Rhonda on the back seat, would squash against her on right turns and slip toward Paul on lefts. Each slide into Rhonda got him a not too feminine elbow and a "your own side, buddy" with a short laugh.

"You've got the notebook?" Rhonda went through her checklist. "You're sure the guy who has connections is here?"

"Here." Fred pointed at the back of his pants where he had the notebook tucked into a new pair of whities. "And Jake, the guy we want, is in. He's always in on Tuesdays. That's walk-in day for lost vets."

The bus pulled into the turnaround across from City College. The trio unloaded through the back door shooing away a student selling bus passes that had been run covertly through the class printing press that morning. Paul and Rhonda watched as Fred took off the wrong way, toward Beeps, the walkup burger joint across the street. He headed toward the thirty-foot neon sign that showed a flashing satellite straight out of the fifties, back when the scientists could do no more than send a beeping signal back to earth.

"Mr. No-Burger, Mr. Anti-Fred. What's happened to you." Paul called to Fred already halfway across the road.

"Beeps serves gourmet cow. Can't deny a gourmet cow or she gets angry."

Fred grabbed a burger at the window and shuffled back to the group with his face nestled in the wrapper."

"Got to build up my strength. I'm the one meeting Jake. I'm the bait and I want to be tasty like my Ms. Cowparts here in the wrapper."

"You're adding onions to your base of patchouli. Jake might jump out the window for fresh air when you walk in." Rhonda had gotten used to the normal smells of Fred's incense days but was not one for onion breath.

"You know the plan?" said Rhonda, focused on the job ahead.

"Yep, you two are here to keep me from backing out, and I'm here to tell Jack about the notebook and flash it at him."

"You got the right notebook?"

"Yep, the red one." Fred pulled it out and double checked. Not trusting Fred to get the right notebook, Rhonda had insisted that the new notebook be a different color from the original black. Fred chose red."

"And you stamped every page?"

"Yes, mam—TOP SECRET everywhere."

Fred had learned to make stamps when he was in the army. A big eraser and an X-acto knife could make any stamp, like the FIGMOs and FUBARs that covered the daily bulletins back in his barracks when he was doing his GI time.

"This book has enough screwy math and drawings and graphs to lure in anyone who's not a true rocket scientist. Ready for duty." Fred wiped the catsup off his chin and faced the school, looking like the buildings might collapse on him any second. He was not a brave man.

Walking to the Veterans' room,
Knowing that I'll meet my doom,
Praying jail is not for me,
Hoping for a life that's free.

The group walked around the drive, looking up at the big science building with its rooftop telescope and observatory that could see nothing but fog most evenings. Behind the main buildings, a set of one-story, wooden World War II leftovers lined the drive. The middle one had a hand-painted sign, "Vets Against War." Fred climbed the steps, avoiding a longhaired couple—the man had taken off his fatigue jacket as he gave the woman a backrub in an early start to a pre-coupling ritual.

Broken-down sofas and pillows lay around inside. Fred's patchouli and onions were overwhelmed with leftovers of a thousand joints that had seen their last moments in this room.

"Hey, boss man. Hey, Jake. Can we go for a walk?"

Jake was over the edge of paranoid, but with good reasons. The Feds had been infiltrating and listening to every move of his vets' organization. Jake was its heart—a medic who had watched too many die, as he kept winning medals trying to save them in Vietnam. Now the medals hung on a Vietnamese flag. He had changed sides. He sat behind an old metal desk. His hair thick and black hung down limp covering the shrapnel scars on his neck and face He looked up trying to place this short-haired, skin-faced intruder.

"Who are you?"

Fred mouthed his name, rubbed his face where his beard had been, and winked. Jake laughed and got up. The two walked out the door and turned down the hill. Three lawn mowers cut away, making it hard to hear.

"OK, Fred what's the story. Why the bare face and the outfit from Kansas?"

Fred ignored the question and started his pre-notebook spiel, "I know you're not one of the violent types, but…"

Jake laughed pointing his forefinger gun barrels and popping both thumb hammers down.

"Want me to take someone out? I quit that business when they took away my uniform. And why are you dressed like a used-car salesman from Iowa? Keep your voice down, they might be listening."

"I'm Fred incognito. The FBI has me in their crosshairs for the lab bombing, and I was just a bystander. But I have something the guys who did it might want. They dropped it when the bombing went down."

He reached behind his back and started to pull out the notebook.

"Don't show it to me here. They probably have binoculars on us."

It was true that the FBI was watching that day from a room in the big admin building. They snapped a picture of Fred.

"A returning vet?" one of the agents monitoring the pair asked. "His hair is too short to be anything else. Draft dodgers all look like hippies these days."

"Maybe a deserter?" the second agent said.

"No resources to chase him now. You stay here with the camera and see what you can get, and I'll see what Jake is doing when he goes back inside the vet building." The second agent slipped out of the admin building. He wore a fatigue jacket, had long hair and was smoking a tobacco roll-up. And his ankles were crusty. He had undercover life down pat.

Jake led Fred into a shed on the edge of the field and tugged the light chain. Fred stood beside an assortment of shovels and rakes as he pulled out the notebook and handed it to Jake. Jake flipped it open and scanned a few pages.

"Here take my card and call me if you know anyone who wants it." Fred handed him one of the cards he had made with his name and Rhonda's message machine number.

"I didn't see the book. Put it back and go home. The Feds probably saw you and will be on your ass before you get across campus."

"OK, you got number one. Now we do the Trots," Paul announced as the threesome entered the large college building on the hill in front of the vets shack.

"Room 301. Go get 'em, Fred. We'll meet you at the bus turnaround."

Paul and Rhonda gave Fred a hug as though he were off on a to-die-for mission. Fred saluted and double stepped up to the third floor.

Goin' to see a Troskyite
Hoping that this fish will bite,
Salivating o'er each page
Like he is a bibliophage.

Fred knocked on the door, looking at pictures of Che and Trotsky tacked over a listing of Mr. Puddingstone's office hours. A cartoon showed Nixon with his pants down getting a whacking from a group of muscular workers.

"It's open."

Fred walked in. The walls had old Soviet posters from the early days just after the Bolshevik revolution. The bookcase was filled with Marx and Lenin. A red star sat on Puddingstone's desk. He wore a cheap suit, not much different from Fred's Salvation Army special. His hair was short and to the point. His glasses, wireframed and functional—Trotsky style. Puddingstone was thin and bookish, not a worker with big arms like in the posters. He taught philosophy always pointing out to his students that he had big frontal lobes, better than biceps.

"Professor Puddingstone, I need to talk to you. Someplace private."

Puddingstone nodded as though this happened often and the two headed down the hall to the men's john. Puddingstone flushed three toilets and ran all the sinks.

"OK, noisy enough. What is it?" he said quietly.

"I'm a student, Fred Arnold, and I was at the bombing at the lab, just walking around minding myself when it went off, and I found something, something that the guys who did it might want."

"I had nothing to do with tha…"

"I know you wouldn't do anything violent."

Puddingstone laughed. "You don't know me then."

"Well, I didn't mean to say you were involved, but you might get out the word about what I have."

Fred pulled out the fake red notebook and opened it. Puddingstone took it and looked.

"Maybe I should keep this. I have a safe place."

"No, I need it back. I told other people about it, and they might get back to me."

Fred grabbed the notebook and turned to leave. He worried Puddingstone might try to take it and rushed the door tossing a card with his name and Rhonda's number toward stall number two.

"That card has how to get me. Thanks, Professor Puddingstone. Got to go," he shouted as he pushed the door to the hallway open.

Thursday Afternoon, Later

"Two down, one to go," Paul said as he gave Fred a hug. Rhonda hugged his other side. Fred needed it. He was shaking in his socks after Mr. Trots.

"Puddingstone is scary, ready to lead the revolution, and I'm not a comrade, more like a kulak up against the wall. I thought he was going to take the book."

"Quit showing off. We know you took Russian history and know the fancy words." Rhonda said.

"Don't worry. He'll spread the word and then we're out of the FBI jam," Paul said trying to encourage Fred. "On to the Maoists."

The three hopped a near empty streetcar and headed toward the center of the city. They huddled in the back on the long wide seat, passing Beeps and the old theater that had decided religion was its true calling. Ocean Ave had become a main thoroughfare and its non-stop traffic was killing the mom-and-pops. An empty lot proclaimed it would be the new Safeway's home, but it wouldn't save the street—customers would come and go, never seeing any of the small shops. The only thing that saved the street from total death was its low rents. Strange shops popped open, but never blossomed, and they died. Non-profits found refuge, and street people found a doorway the rain couldn't reach.

The streetcar clunked down toward the ocean, not reaching it but turning when it neared the monied hills where streets had columns announcing their names and private guards roaming in well-marked cars. The streetcar turned again to snail through a smart block of coffee shops and banks. It hit the tunnel and after ten dark minutes arrived at Market and Castro, a working-class neighborhood with a big theater and Fred's secret Swedish restaurant hiding two blocks away. Then down Market until they transferred, catching the 14 Mission back toward the Chew where Paul and Fred had chomped down their post-lab burgers only two days ago.

> *Riding on my seated ass,*
> *I want to walk upon the grass,*
> *And feel my feet as they make haste.*
> *Buses are a giant waste*
> *Of time.*

"Christ, I could have walked here and back. Now you know why taking the bus hurts your soul. We've been riding forty-five minutes. You need to exercise your feet in this city, not dumb around on the Muni."

"Are you finished, Fred." Rhonda gave him the look.

"We're here." Paul cut in and pulled the cord.

"Next Stop" lit over the driver's head and a bell rang. The bus pulled halfway into the stop, six feet from the curb.

Fred bounded out, Paul was more deliberate as he stepped down, and Rhonda checked to see if they left anything.

"Paul and I'll get a coffee. Report back when you have mission accomplished."

Rhonda gave Fred a gentle push toward the bookstore filled with posters of plump ducks swimming and matching plump peasant-looking types smiling. Paul walked into the bookstore.

"Is the manager in?"

The clerk had a tight black bun on her head, a plump face, plump as the ducks in the poster, loose blue pants, the ubiquitous blue padded jacket, and black cloth shoes, almost mary-janes, direct from China on her feet. She pointed toward the back. She held up her little red book of the Chairman's thoughts and nodded like Fred should get one. He pulled out his larger red TOP SECRET notebook and waved it at her as he walked toward the manager. The clerk looked at Fred's book but didn't smile. Recent converts were serious about their new religion even if it had no upstairs god.

"Who are you?" the manager asked as she took the big red book. She looked like an older clone of the upfront clerk.

"Fred Arnold, at your service." He pulled out his last card with his name and Rhonda's phone number and handed it to her.

She thumbed the book open and stared at the big TOP SECRET stamp on the top of each page. Then she started to tuck the notebook into one of her pockets.

"That's just for looking. Thought you might know someone who needs it."

"And you are looking for money?

"No, just friends."

Fred gripped the notebook, pulled it away from her, and shoved it back under his belt. He pushed it down the front of his pants, more polite, he thought than in the back. The manager watched closely.

"What do you want."

"Just to get this back to the notebook's owner. The owner dropped it. He'll know who it is. It happened at the lab explosion."

"I have no idea what you're talking about. Now get your honky ass and your grifter bullshit out of here or you'll meet the wrath of the workers." She'd slipped back into an earlier vocabulary incarnation, speaking street talk but ending with a dash of Mao.

Fred hustled out the door and met his partners at the coffee shop, stopping first to grab a big round one, jelly-filled, to go with yet another cup of coffee."

"Not easy to dunk, but worth it."

Fred sighed as he bit into the coffee-laden, soggy creature he was holding, only to squirt a stream of red jelly toward Rhonda.

"Forget the donut, mister, how was your mission?"

"Complete. Book displayed, card handed out—and still in one piece. The Trots are serious—skinny, nasty, and serious, but the chunky Maoists look like they would cut you down without a thought."

"Back to the hotel? Red still holding down the fort?"

"I bet he's in the lobby watching TV with the alkies and the walker-creeping crowd."

Thursday Evening

> *Sitting hungry, tired, and weary*
> *Bad guys in this myst-er-ear-ee*
> *Badest gonna shoot me dead.*
> *Say goodbye to your friend Fred.*

Fred looked walleyed, dazed, and down as he stared at the still-unopened pizza box sitting on Rhonda's red carry-on. Paul and Fred sat cross-legged on the floor; Red and Rhonda hunched forward on the bed.

"How long do we wait to start dinner?" Fred asked to the ceiling as he looked up at the dead bugs in the light fixture over their heads.

Red jumped in, "If you got something important in that book, you'll hear real soon. Don't worry. It's what you gonna do when they call that you should be thinking about. You're the bait and bait don't live long unless it's one smart little fishy. Remember that." Then he spit from the side of his mouth into the coffee can sitting next to the wall.

When the threesome had returned to the room and found Red napping, Fred woke him to share his adrenaline high. He bubbled out, not with song and rhyme, but with a short version of the story: three suspects, the big red book, and the dangling Fred bait. Red had listened, shaking his head, saying, "You're looking for it, boy. You now have three more after your San Francisco butt. Not just the cops. You ain't going to make it long enough to worry about an old man's pains like I got."

"I need pizza to help me think. Let's open that baby." Fred was reviving from the low dudgeon that Red had dumped on him. As the cheese and pepperoni molecules wafted through the close air of the room, he felt a new rush of appetite-based adrenaline surging from his overworked glands. He pulled the box lid open, reached in, and cradled a slice in his right hand, just as a bear would hold some large delight from a dumpster. "Anyone else?" he said a second before his mouth was too full for word or song.

"You have to meet them somewhere, give them the red book, and say you want to join up. You're a revolutionary in your soul and you want to jump start your career with a high-profile outfit, like theirs. Then you go to their location and let us know where. We clue in the FBI and case closed." Paul had worked it out.

"We'll need to rescue Fred before the Feds arrive," Rhonda argued back. "And how're we going to do that? If we don't, the FBI'll come in with guns blazing. They don't want to go to trial. They want the case dead and gone. Mostly dead. And I want to keep my Fred alive and free from nasty bullet holes. I'm sentimental that way."

"I want to stay live bait, not some dead nightcrawler hooked by the Trots or Maoists. The FBI doesn't give you a bye if you joined to help the government team. Rhonda's right. I'll get choice, grade A, bullets in me for my efforts if I'm there when the FBI kicks in the door. Let's think more."

Red had been sitting still. "Well, back in my day, we fired buckshot their way. That slowed 'em down. Maybe we follow Fred and give them a taste of country living."

No one paid attention. Red didn't seem to care but spit his tobacco juice hard enough to make the can ring.

"OK, you hand over the book. Then clear out. We follow them back to their hideout. Sound better?" Rhonda had a worried look on her face. "At least we can get pictures of them when you meet, even if they get away from us."

"So, do you want to call the answering machine now and see who bit? We need to get started." Paul liked to change the subject when times were difficult, or when he wasn't in charge. Fred and Rhonda had taken over the planning, well mostly Rhonda, and Paul saw they were right in protecting Fred, but he wanted to get in on basement-level planning. His new lab job depended on doing this book drop right and clearing Fred and, most importantly, himself.

"Let's just eat." Fred looked at his mostly-gone pizza slice. The others looked at Fred.

"Well, it looks like you boys—'scuse me ma'am—have this as under control as you're going to get it, and I don't seem to be adding much with my scattergun theories, and my grandbaby girl phoned here at the hotel today and wants me back at the commune, so I think I'll head on up north. You got the room two more nights, Fred—all on me, all paid in advance. Stop by sometime—and you two, make sure you save that nasty smelling skin of his."

Red had never mentioned the Fred's smell before. He picked up his suitcase and walked out.

"I think we hurt his feelings," Fred said.

"Maybe, but it simplifies things," Rhonda said breaking the silence after the door closed. Now I only have you two to take care of."

FRIDAY

Friday Afternoon

"No messages. Twenty-four hours and nothing. The word's out so we should be hearing something." Fred was reporting back after he had gone out, walked a mile to the bay, and used a pay phone to call the message machine. Nothing.

They spent another night in the hotel. Fred had his own room now that Red had pulled up stakes, but he didn't use it after wiling his way into Rhonda's. After the night of bed-thumping, they spent the next day in Fred's room, bored and hungry for action and food. Paul wandered over about noon.

"Patience, it takes time for the word to spread. And we still don't have our plans in place," Rhonda said.

"I'm going batty in here and watching the TV in the lobby is worse. We've got to do something." Paul was looking out the window but seeing nothing but the grey foggy day as he spoke.

"We're hiding out, remember?" Rhonda explained once again to the men why they were locked in the room looking at the desiccated remains of yesterday's pizza.

"OK, let's hide out somewhere else for a while."

"I can go out. I'm the well-disguised Not-Fred, but you two are still Paul and Rhonda. We need to modify you into mutants, like me."

"Women can mutate anytime. Hair, clothes, a whole new person. But Paul is the one we need to do a little surgery on."

"Get me a wheelchair. Wrap me in a blanket. I'll drool. And put a shawl over my head. I'll be a wheelchair mutant. Just get me out of here."

"Paul, that's stupid. Everyone would notice. We need to make you as invisible as a hairball in a cat house."

"I'll buy clothes for you, for all of us. Full-tourist drag. Rhonda and I can be siblings out with our Cousin Paul, out on a holiday. And do some hot chocolate at Ghirardelli."

"Sick 'em, Fred. Get us clothes. Mutate us," Paul said smiling.

"We've only been here one day. I know Fred has done more time locked in with Red, but do we need to go out?" Rhonda wanted to lie low in the room and call out for food. But she wouldn't mind a clean bathroom—the communal one for the floor was disgusting.

"It'll be safe. We'll need to be different people, that's all. If I am the Not-Fred, then you can be the Not-Paul and Not-Very-Rhonda.

"OK, call me big sis and don't come knocking on my door tonight. I don't do family night," Rhonda said as she punched Fred in the shoulder.

"Give me sizes. I'll make you into tourists from Omaha. That's about as unnoticeable to the FBI as you can get.

Fred took the elevator and walked a block to the Salvation Army store. In the neighborhood around the hotel, if you could call it a neighborhood where your neighbors were as likely to mug you as to say hello, there were cheap shops: Saint Vincent's, Goodwill, and the Salvation Army. The miracle mile for used clothes and scuffed shoes.

Friday Evening

I'm a tourist from old Mizzou
Flew in United, havin' a do.
Seein' the sites with Sis and Cuz,
Irish coffee and a headshop buzz.

The three walked through the tenderloin arm-in-arm
doing a Strawman-Dorothy-Lion dance, singing and gliding past
the corner liquor stores, peep shows, and porno shops. Fred and
Paul gawked properly as anyone from Omaha should, acting too
nervous and self-righteous to go in and have a full-size peek as
long as a lady was around.

"We ought to go into acting."

"You have a grand notion of yourself, Paul. You're just
an Omaha prude at heart," Rhonda said. "That's not acting. It's
the true Paul bursting forth."

Paul played his part in a checkered, stiff collar shirt and
a pair of pleated suit pants with a one-inch cuff. A trench coat
covered his ensemble. "It was on sale," was all Fred could say
when Rhonda asked about how the coat fit into Midwest drag.

"He looks a private dick, 1930s' style, not a farm boy
special."

Fred still wore the suit Red had supplied but with the
lapels turned up to warm his neck in the San Francisco evening
chill. Goodwill had provided him a hand painted tie—Sunset
over Tahiti—wide enough to reach from ear to ear if the wind
flipped it across his face, which it did as they walked or rather
skipped down the street. Rhonda wore a flowery print dress,

hanging down to the knees and a little past. "My mother had one of these and a car coat like this, too," she said as she dressed for the night flipping her black straight hair into an appropriate non-coastal bun. They looked more hippie-weird than Midwest tourist, but no one seemed to notice, even as they continued their song and dance taking the whole sidewalk.

> *We're the team that rules the night.*
> *We sing and dance and are a sight.*
> *We do the streets; we do the walk.*
> *We watch them locals gape and gawk.*

"What are you trying to do." Paul said. "You're Fredding again with your nonsense songs spilling out. Get back into your yahoo Midwest character and give that panhandler a quarter for a coffee like your farmboy mama told you to—be good to the downtrodden and charitable to the sick or some such. And remember that singing is only for church on Sunday."

"That's your commie 'share the wealth' idea, not my mama's. She was a family-first Christian, God helps those… Damn, we're coming up on the Fed building, where they keep the FBI under wraps. They have cameras. I'm going down to Market Street. Too many unfond memories up here."

The trio turned and headed toward the subway-construction desolation of Market.

"We need a dose of the Fillmore," Fred said as he tried wagging his head but without his full mop of hair he looked like a deranged Midwesterner, not a hippie.

"Yes, a little dose will do you," Paul chimed in.

"The Fillmore is one bad idea. We're hiding out. How can we hide out in there with the music and noise and God-knows-who watching?" Rhonda shook her head.

"Easy, It's dark. And everyone watches the light show or the band. We'll be as anonymous as a Polish polka in Poughkeepsie., Paul had perked up at the idea of going out to the Fillmore.

"No funny stuff. No licking paper squares, no brownies, no capsules, no tabs, no joints, no alcohol. We stay on our toes. And keep on gawking like you just left the farm."

We are straight, straight from Poughkeepsie
Doing Polkas in the street.
We love them accord-i-on-es,
And dancing with our farmboy feet.

They each took an apple at the door and ate as they went upstairs to find seats far to the side, deep in the darkness. The Airplane doing full-bore, pulsed power chords throbbed the walls. The air moved in time with the bass. Giant red amoebas squished in and out over bubbles of green and blue projected on the far wall. The light show covered a space the size of a house. A mirrored ball spun in the center of the hall sending light rays streaming. Some dancers followed the lights, others the music. The musicians yelled; the speakers upped the volume to near-death levels. The lights turned colors and the room turned into a rainbow. The room went black, and strobes flashed. Dancers became jerky, twitching bodies. They spun strings of beads over their heads in time with the flashes, making the strands dance, floating in the air as the light caught the beads at the top of their swings. A new couple swished in, he in a tux and she in a gown. Her diamonds sparkled in the lights. They did some swing jitterbugging learned in a big-bucks Arthur Murray Studio. Pacific Heights had come for its noblesse oblige moment. After a few minutes they were drowned in bodies as more hit the floor. Sweat flew from all; the inner patchouli of the women was awakened, but the men just smelled. Everyone swirled. Everyone sped up their movements. The band obliged with a faster and faster and faster beat.

"I'm going to dance." Paul stood.

Rhonda stood in front blocking him. "You dance and you'll blow your cover. Midwestern men don't dance; they rope cattle. But, I forgot, you can't dance worth anything. Just do your yokel stomp out there. That'll be fine. Like some cornhusker who was slipped some acid."

Paul shook and twisted and raised his arms. He finally found something near the beat.

Fred grabbed Rhonda.

"OK, but let's stay back here," she said and the two stood near their chairs and twisted semi-serpentine as they circled Paul. Fred's scents started mixing flavors pulled up from deep in his skin as he sweated with his white-boy efforts. For an hour, the band played with no break until finally the guitars hit one last chord that rang for a minute. The crowd yelled for more even as some collapsed on the floor.

"Whew. I think we've freed ourselves from the funk of this bombed out book chase. Music does that." Paul could never stop analyzing."

"I think we're crazy, dancing when we're nothing but FBI bait." Rhonda yelled over the din. "But we're no longer from Kansas where they worry about things like that."

Everyone from Kansas state who comes to the big city
Says they crazy in this town, then they hear my ditty.
We not crazy, we just free, we be dancing fools
When you go home remember that
and you'll be oh so cool.

"No one says cool anymore, Fred. How about 'you'll be oh so trippy.'"

"You take over as the songwriter, Paul, and I'll take your job as the hot freaky throwback dancer."

"Down Fred. Don't be sensitive. We know you worked a long time on those lyrics."

Rhonda gave Fred a consolation kiss and waved Paul away. Paul got drinks. The three sat exhausted.

"Enough." Rhonda stood and took Fred's arm. "Let's went, as Pancho used to say to the Cisco Kid."

The three exited—Paul with a bit of physical urging from Fred—and headed back to Market.

"I want to sack out. And soon," Rhonda yawned.

"I'm ready when you are."

"Fred, I'm going to sleep. You keep your ideas to yourself tonight. Maybe I'll invite you over in the morning if you're a good boy and go straight to your room and say your prayers."

Paul followed the pair out the door. Fred put his arm around Rhonda as she walked with a sag back toward the Tenderloin. Fred listed sideways. Only Paul had some of his daytime snap.

"Let's check the answering machine while we have some time." Paul took a dime out of his pocket as he neared a pay phone. He called Rhonda's number.

"What's your playback code?" Paul yelled.

"Fourteen hundred and ninety-two."

Paul punched in the numbers and waited while the tape rewound. He listened as it started playing.

"Your sister wonders where you are," Paul called out to Rhonda.

"She always wonders. She wonders why I'm here and not back East. I wonder the opposite for her. Why vegetate on the East Coast when you can vegetate here. That's what I'm doing as soon as I can tonight."

"Hey," Paul yelled. "This is it. I'll replay. What numbers do a rewind?"

Rhonda took over the phone and punched the star button. The answering machine's recorder whirred as it rewound and then first played her sister's message again. Finally, the next message started:

"Got the word you found my book. I think I dropped it on the bus. My lab book, right? I have a reward for you. Meet me right now, if you can, or tomorrow at Green Apple Books. Let's say noon. In the numerology section. My name is Charlie. Thanks."

Rhonda wrote "Charlie, Green Apple, noon" on her hand.

"What's this bus crap? He knows where he dropped it." Paul said. "And what's with the politeness. He sounds like my mother."

"He can't say he dropped it at the lab," said Rhonda. "You know who is probably listening in. The FBI has big ears. Now, what's the plan?"

"You know the plan. You made it up," Fred said looking at her.

"OK, you check out numerology in the Green Apple tomorrow. Find our man. give him the book, then clear out. Paul and I follow whoever it is until we find out where his gang is staying and what they're doing. Then we decide about turning them in or letting them publish. That's the plan, right?"

"You forgot the part about getting the FBI off my back. That's the most important.

> *Catch a fishie on the hookie.*
> *Bait it with a big red bookie.*
> *Free old Freddie from the Feds.*
> *Make him happy, not too dead.*

"I'm going to call the bookstore and ask for Charlie." Fred said.

Paul gave him a nod and then a dime. Fred looked it up in the directory and dialed. The three crowded around the phone receiver. It rang once. It rang ten more times. Then the scratchy voice of a recording machine came on.

"Green Apple Books. We're open ten to ten. Call back tomorrow or leave a message."

"Christ, it's tomorrow already," Phil looked at his watch.

Fred hung up.

"Why not just surprise him. I know the store," Rhonda said.

"I like surprises," Fred agreed, and Paul nodded.

"Now let's get back. Otherwise, I curl up to sleep right here on the sidewalk and you guys stand watch."

They retraced their earlier path. The porno shops and liquor stores were busier. Bodies skulked back and forth. Sirens sounded a block away. Someone screamed. A normal night in the Tenderloin.

The hotel had half its neon sign lit. The other half died years back if the pigeon droppings on the sign's broken glass tubing were any gauge. Fred and Rhonda lugged themselves to the door. Their hide-out life and a lack of caffeine had them ready to drop.

The front desk was lit brightly for a change. The clerk became animated when he saw Fred, acting as if he was finally taking his job seriously.

"Take this and tell your friends to stay out."

Paul stepped up. "What friends? You mean us?" Paul put his arm around Rhonda

"No, I mean the ones who were here with the Mao-crap clothes and the baseball bats under their blue coat padding. They were here twice. The first time they left the envelope and the second they threatened me. I don't do bullshit like this. I babysit my hotel alkies who hide their bottles and watch the lobby TV and pay their rent when the welfare check comes in."

The clerk tossed the envelope on the counter and turned away mumbling, "Maybe you should go someplace where folk like you belong."

Fred and Rhonda looked at each other. Fred spoke up, "He's right we're too high class for this dump."

Paul ripped the envelope open. A polaroid fell to the floor. Red was smiling in garish Polaroid colors. Two blue-jacketed, Maoist arms wrapped around him, holding him up. Paul snatched up the photo and started reading the back.

"Want your gramps back? Leave the book with the clerk. NOW."

"Shit," Fred called out then lowered his voice. "They think Red's my grandpop."

"Who cares? They kidnapped him. We need to get him back. They might ship him off to Peking," Rhonda replied. "We have two big nibbles on one fake book. Maybe we do a Solomon and chop it in two?"

"We can't give them the book. It'll go straight to some scientists in China." Paul argued. "And then the world will have even more neutron bombs. And we'll be shot as spies."

"Not the real book, stupid. The fake red one."

It took some explaining and yelling but the clerk agreed to handoff the book, finally understanding that facing a baseball bat emptyhanded was more dangerous than having his hands full with the red book.

"So, what do we do about the guy who called, the one we see tomorrow at the bookstore?"

"We don't know which one of these is the real bomber. We need to check both of them. We made one fake book. We'll make another. But for now, we wait and watch. I want to see these well-padded thugs and see if they're the real thing." Rhonda had perked up to full alert level, giving orders. Fred lingered in his late-night fugue. Paul danced around like the boxers on Red's TV a few days earlier. The clerk hid in the back room.

"OK, positions, everyone." Rhonda called out. They had their plan to catch the Mao thugs. Rhonda took her spot across from the hotel in a doorway. She didn't want the kidnappers to notice her waiting, so she hiked up her dress and fit right in with the women on the street, getting offers from cars and passerbys. Paul hid in an alley and popped out when she needed backup. Fred sat in the hotel's back room behind the clerk singing away:

> *Way down upon the Yangtse River,*
> *Far, far away,*
> *That's where my notebook longs to live, or*
> *Maybe it just wants to play.*

"You did a great job selling Fred to the clerk," Paul said to Rhonda who wandered out from her doorway toward him.

"Fred makes for great protection. The clerk just needed convincing that Fred was a real he-guy who could put the lights out for the Maoists."

"Fred couldn't protect himself from a pussycat."

"But he's our hero, putting himself on the line to be the bait. Remember they know him, not us."

"If he's on the line then why're we on the street while he's inside warm and safe."

They shut up when two men entered the hotel: one plump filling out his padded jacket with muscles, the other with a baseball bat under his armpit. Louisville Slugger poked itself out when the jacket slipped off his shoulder every few seconds.

"You got it?" The fat one asked the clerk.

The clerk laid the red book on the counter and walked to the back room. Fred slid further out of view.

The two took the book, looked in it for a second, then exited through the front door. A car pulled up, an old sedan with a broken headlight, and the two piled in.

Paul looked at Rhonda. "What do we do?"

"What do you think? We grab a cab and follow them."

Rhonda waved at passing cabs as the sedan pulled farther away. Finally, one stopped, and they jumped in the back seat.

"Follow that sedan at the traffic light." Paul yelled to the driver.

"What do you think this is, bub? The movies? Tell me where you want to go. That's what me and the cab do."

"I want to go where that car's going."

The black sedan turned.

"What car? I don't see no car."

Paul and Rhonda jumped out and ran toward the corner. The sedan was gone. The cab wasn't. "You got in the cab, I hit the meter, you pay the fare."

Paul shut him up with two bucks and turned to Rhonda, "Well that was a good plan, following them when we had no wheels."

"If they'd been walking, we'd have been fine."

"I don't think kidnappers walk or take the bus, Rhonda. Let's find Fred."

Walking back toward the hotel, they heard footsteps coming up from behind. Rhonda got ready to run, Paul turned.

"Well, if it ain't Rhonda and little what's-his-name. Both of them all dolled up and ready for a night out. What's old stay-at-home Fred going to say. Why the heck are you out here and not back hiding out in the hotel?"

It was Red.

"Red, what are you doing here?"

They had forgotten. The red book was a trade for Red. And Red was back, a bit ruffled, but alive and chewing hard on his tobacco wad, smelling like alcohol.

"Red, you're OK. Did the kidnappers treat you right?"

"Kidnappers, I met some old boys who took me for a drink yesterday. I figured that granddaughter of mine could do without me for a few more days. What a drink. It knocked me for a loop and a long nap and now they just brought me back here.

"But they said…"

Fred came running out of the building when he saw Red and gave him a big hug, one that Red tried to squeeze out of.

"We love you, Red. Welcome home."

Red pulled back remembering the smells that came attached to Fred, trying to air himself out.

Friday Late Night

We're awaiting on the baddies
hump your swagger, little laddies.
Don't let no wicked baseball bat
Knock you silly, knock you flat.

They sat in Paul's room for a powwow. Fred brought the pillow from his room across the hall and was lying on the floor next to Paul. Red and Rhonda sat on the bed.

"Well, what now? We have the Maoists after us and someone at the Green Apple looking for us tomorrow. One of them is fake and didn't steal the book from the lab. But which one?" Paul asked.

"It's after midnight, we're tired enough to die, and no one has come for us yet, so I say we sleep on it." Fred said.

"The Maoists know where we are, and when they figure out the notebook is a fake, they're coming back. I say we check out of the hotel and keep an eye on the place from someplace safe. And get a car so we don't lose them next time. But first someplace safe for when they find out the book is a fake."

"Calm down Rhonda, it's late and no one's going to…"

Someone beat on Fred's door across the hall. Then the door gave in with a crash. Paul motioned for quiet, but he didn't need to. The others were stock-still. Paul stood and looked out the peek-hole in the door. "It's them. The Mao guys," he whispered. Red picked up his walking stick and held it ready for a belly jab or an eye poke if anyone came in, Rhonda looked for anything that could be a weapon. She grabbed an ash tray. Fred and Paul started to push the dresser against the door, but its legs screeched, so they stopped and looked towards Red and Rhonda.

Paul went back to watching through the peek-hole and saw a bed turned over into the hall and a dresser dumped in Fred's room.

"Where you think that guy went. His clothes are here," A voice yelled down the hall.

Fred sidled next to Paul and listened with his ear against the door.

One of the men trashing the room yelled out, "We wait downstairs. He'll come back for his stuff sometime. Then we find out what he's trying to pull. He gave us his I-was-at-the-bombing-story. This time we don't take the old man, we take the dude who tried to pass the book off. We take him for a trip."

The four in Paul's room listened to the steps moving down the hall and then to a door closing. Finally, Red pulled open the hall door, holding his walking stick like a fungo bat.

"Nobody in the hall," he whispered as Fred and Rhonda tried to pull him back in the room. "These boys want you, Fred. And they sounded like the ones that took me drinking. Maybe doped me up a little. You got one big nibble on that red book bait of yours."

"Fleabag Arms, farewell. It's time to part." Fred headed across the hall and gathered up an armful of clothes that lay scattered on the floor."

"Fire escape?" Fred asked.

"Fire escape." The others replied.

The hotel had two. One came down in front of the

hotel, the other in a back alley. Front was not an option with the Mao crew waiting, so the four headed to the back window and an ancient ironwork balcony with burned down butts scattered everywhere showing its true purpose—a terrace for smokers.

Red pulled open the window. "Looks shaky. Start with the lightest, then work our way to Fred."

"Good idea," Paul said as climbed through the window and started down the metal steps at the side of the balcony.

"I'm lighter than you—me first," Rhonda called down.

"I want to check out the alley, and I'm not that much heavier."

Paul made it to the second floor and then stepped on the drop-down ladder. Its counterweight broke free and he rode gliding to the ground.

"Come on. No one's here."

But a body in the alley rolled over and got to its knees.

"He's just sleeping it off next to the dumpster. Come on," Paul whispered loudly to the crew who had made it down to the second floor.

Rhonda rode the drop-down to the ground, followed by Red. Fred was close behind.

The drunk stood shakily and approached Fred. "Buddy, got a dollar."

"You're late for the party. Go back to sleep." But Fred handed over a dollar and aimed the body back at the dumpster. It had other ideas and turned down a side alley toward the front of the building, stumbling and looking hard at his new dollar bill.

"Shit. The Mao team will want to check this back area if he walks out front."

"Which way? This is your town. I'm a tar heel Carolinian, so someone get us out of here."

Paul and Rhonda walked briskly away from the hotel. They came out on O'Farrell where neons burned in reds and yellows and peep shows ran full blast, but the street was almost empty except for one group just coming around a corner. Fred saw its leader, Puddingstone, the prof from City College. The Trots were on the way. Not to save the day, Fred thought.

"Back in the alley. We've got company looking for me, and the Trots and Maoists don't play well together. This may lead to fireworks. Other way."

They crossed behind the hotel again and went in the other direction past spilled dumpsters and piles of garbage. More sleeping bodies huddled in doorways. No one stirred as they passed.

Yelling started in front of the hotel. "Fucking Trots. I should've known you were behind this"

"What're you doing here? Wrong path Maoists. You got that notebook? It's ours."

The yelling got louder. Fred and friends ran toward Van Ness. Sirens zeroed in on the hotel. The Maoists and Trots zeroed in on each other.

"We need to find a place for the night. It's cold and the crazies are out," Rhonda called to the group."

"Follow me. I know a place," Fred said, "And you don't have to buy a meal or coffee to keep your seat. You can even sleep there."

SATURDAY

Saturday Morning, 2 AM

The orange plastic chair kept Fred awake so he spent an hour watching clothes spinning in the dryer. Rhonda and Paul had nodded off with their heads on the big table for folding clothes. A tie-dyed local was sleeping on the bay window ledge; his dog slept tied to a clothes cart.

"I'm an old man and I'm doing better than you." Red nudged Fred. "How many times you dried the clothes now?"

"You've got to be doing clothes or the cops hassle you."

"But why other people's clothes?"

"They were already here. It's cheaper than renting a room."

"And so comfortable," Red said as he looked to see if Rhonda or Paul were stirring.

"It's this or the coffee shop. And here your bladder gets a break. You got to do a cup every hour in a coffee joint if you want to keep a seat. And you can't sleep there. Here you can. Well, some people can. But you're right. Let's go get a cup."

Fred scrawled a few lines on a laundry soap box turned inside out and stuck it under Rhonda's arm. She moaned but did not move."

"See you, beautiful."

"Screw you, Fred." Rhonda half opened her eyes and waved feebly as Fred and Red walked out the door.

"Ah, the comforts of the local laundromat for them and for us, thank God, the all-night donut shop," Fred said as the pair walked down Haight.

"Thank God for laundromats that let you stick your head in the dryer to keep warm," Red said laughing.

"I only did that twice."

They sat on stools in the Dirty Donut, another of the old school, low-brow joints that had not deserted the Haight when the hippies arrived. The head shops and spiritual bookstores and crystal mystic readings would let anyone hang around all day and maybe have a smoke, but they were all closed. The trusty donut shop took all comers, early or late, and dosed them with caffeine, not LSD.

"Your plans worked well, young man. Maybe too well. Everyone's after you. You going to report 'em all to the FBI?" Red laughed again.

"Be serious."

"I'm too old for that. You backed yourself in a hell of a corner."

"OK, but we attracted suspects—and I bet one is the real thing, the one that blew the lab. I'm still waiting because no one has said anything about the book's color being wrong. That's what I'm counting on. When someone asks for the black notebook, then I've got their number. I'll ring their bell and sic the FBI on their ding-dong asses."

"You really going to turn them in to the Feds? I thought you were one of those red-eyed radicals."

"I just want this over. How else can I end it?"

"I'll tell you one thing—turning someone in isn't going to end it for you. You'll just be on everyone's shit list if you do that. And the FBI will still think you were in on it."

"What would you do, Red."

"High tail it to the hills. That's all you can do sometimes. Or get your prison suit washed and ironed. Looks like that's where you're heading. Unless one of these groups gets real pissed off. Then get your funeral suit dry cleaned."

Fred choked on his coffee. Red laughed again.

"That's a joke, son. You got to learn life's tough. It's not some hippie la-la world like up on the commune. Life nailed me. Why'd you think I'm here and not sitting with my feet up on my farm? The bank owns it, and I own a suit and a pair of shoes and not much more. You got to think hard on this one you're in, son. Maybe you just pray hard."

Fred reached into the back of his jeans and pulled out the black lab book. "Here you take the notebook, the real one. You look most likely to succeed in any getaway because you don't fit the profile: you're not young, fiery-eyed, and hairy. I trust you. And when I need it, I'll let you know. OK?"

"I got just the place." Red took the notebook and shoved it into a pocket in his coat. "I saw where you kept it, so I'm not going to put it any place I care about. But I'll keep it. And one day you may just live through this and ask for it."

"Don't be a pessimist, Red. Of course, Fred will live through this." Paul said as he and Rhonda walked into the donut shop. He dropped down on a stool next to Red. Rhonda perched herself neatly by Fred.

"I need sleep," Rhonda said.

"We all need sleep, but we have to plan," Paul countered.

"Sleep first, plan later. How can you plan when your brain is on idle. Let's get a room and crash for the day. Someplace safe and then figure this out."

"Anyone know a place to crash here in the Haight?" Paul said looking at Rhonda.

"Anyone can crash anywhere in the Haight, but I need a bed free of crabs, or feet fungi, with nothing crawling, man or insect. And preferably a ladies-only john."

"You three crash for week if you want, but I'm heading to the bookstore today. You aren't on the current number one FBI hit list, not a certified grade A criminal like me. I'm going to have my picture hanging in every post office. I'll make the most wanted. To get this straightened out, I have to strike while my brain is hot."

"Your brain's nothing but a warmed-over sump of shoddy neurons—but we're with you. Right Paul? Right Red? We can take it easy when we're dead." The two nodded. "On to the Green Apple. But it doesn't open 'till noon. We have eight lovely hours to rest somewhere."

"OK, but no more laundromat. I'm going to the Incense Factory and crash there." Fred had given up on hiding out. If the FBI was casing the place, then it was over. But if not they he could sleep. Only Red balked at the idea. He wanted to head for the hills.

They bussed over. No one was watching the place at 4:30 a.m. Fred unlocked the door. He knew that behind the crates of incense direct from India, mixed in with the sacks of yohimbe bark, eucalyptus buttons, an assortment of mushrooms, and God-knows-what, there were some places to crash. Not much, but anything was better than the laundromat.

The smell was strong but the need for sleep was stronger.

The group woke about ten. Red stayed in a chair and slept sitting; the others flopped on old mattresses.

"I need to wash. I smell like Fred. You got a shower? I'm incensed."

"Don't be picky, Paul. The rest rooms have a sink and cold water. And paper towels and a ton—yes, a ton, two thousand pounds—maybe more—of sandalwood soap. Go do it." Rhonda spoke from experience.

"I'm incensed, too. And pissed off. Nothing will wash that feeling off," Fred was trying to work up his anger before he met the bookstore guy.

"A clean neck and some help from God are all you need to succeed." Red got in a few words as they lined up at the sinks in the restroom.

It took a half hour to clean up. They assembled, pink and shiny, at the front ready for an assault on the Green Apple.

"Before we leave, we need to plan a little. Remember last night we were too tired but now we have all brain cells firing." Rhonda had blocked the door and made the three men sit on crates. "We need another fake notebook, and we looked stupid when the Maoists drove off and left us staring at their bumper, trying to grab a cab. We need wheels to follow Fred if they take him away."

"Take me away…?"

Paul perked up. "I was thinking the same thing. And I'm thinking two wheels are the way to go. I can outride anything on the streets here in the city. I run lights. I one-way backwards. I crank for miles and miles. Didn't you say you had a company bike here?

"Yep. For burrito runs." Fred had experience with these.

"I'll take it and beat you to the Green Apple by ten minutes. You have to take the Fillmore bus and transfer to the Clement." Paul started rolling up his right pantleg readying for the ride.

Red added his words of wisdom, "Last one out is a dead possum."

Saturday Noon

Clement Street was going bell-bottomed, becoming a middle-class, revisionist hippiedom. Comedy clubs had opened, a boulangerie was trying to survive, and Busvan, the block-long used furniture store had become the darling of the long hairs. Other old standbys still anchored the street: the Russian deli, the sporting goods store, the grocery with produce stalls rolled out on the sidewalk, and, of course, Hamburger Heaven. The Green Apple was a recent addition that sported a whiff of dope. The straighter part of the street's inhabitants said they smelled the odor of bubbling revolution there, too.

Paul was nervously walking his bike up and down when the bus pulled in. The trio came down its front steps and nodded toward him.

"If we get split up, we do the KSAN check in. Call with where to meet. Just like before." Rhonda said as she gave Fred a farewell hug. Red spat a wad of tobacco and Paul gave a weak wave. Fred shook his head in disbelief at what he was doing and went into the bookstore. The rest retreated into yet another coffee shop and sat looking out the front window, Paul watching the bike and the others watching the Green Apple's front entrance.

"Where's numerology?"

The clerk pointed toward the back of the store. Fred walked past Tarot, Buddhism, and the I Ching, looking for some sign of life. A woman thumbed through a Satanism manual; otherwise, no one. Fred pulled a thick volume from the shelf and faked a read.

Will those yarrow sticks tell me
What to do to keep me free.
And how to keep us all from harm
And catch the nasties with bad karm —— a.

Fred jumped when he felt a tap on his shoulder. "I must be the nasty you want. I think you have my book."

Fred turned and looked into the eyes of the Ferret, his round face framed with neatly trimmed, auburn-toned mutton chops and a top bush of flying hair rivaling Einstein's famous do. His eyes, too close together to be truly human, studied Fred. He looked an old thirty, one living the 1950s, sporting his Ban the Bomb pin and needing only a pipe to finish off his elbow-patched, tweed jacket, professorial look.

Fred smiled and pulled out red book number two, the one that they had just bought as a replacement. Their fake TOP SECRET stamp had done the job again. Rhonda had scribbled in some equations, but the book was mostly empty. Fred hoped Mr. Ferret was only the messenger, not the brain who could see through the deception.

The Ferret opened the book. "OK, what's the game? This isn't mine."

"Tell me about yours and you'll get it."

"Mine is your ticket to healthy living. It's black and thick and what your red book attempts to be."

The Maoists and the Trots had just become just noise. The Ferret, of course, was the real thing. He was the one who had dropped the notebook, right in front of Fred.

"OK. I believe you, but I don't have it with me. You wouldn't believe how many scammers and revolutionaries are after your book. So, I made dummies to make sure I got the right party."

"I'm for real, and game time is over. You *will* call someone to bring it to me."

Fred understood as he looked behind him. Ferret nodded toward two hundred and fifty pounds of meat standing next to the phrenology shelf. It rubbed its shaved head and then cracked its banana-fingered knuckles.

"You don't need the phrenology monster. I'm on your side. Do I look like a pig? Like the fuzz? Can I chant one two three four, I don't want your fucking war? I'm yours. Viva la Revolución."

"I have no idea who you are, but you smell a mess. Even if you're on our side, let's say my big friend here is a guarantee, a guarantee you'll come with us and give us the book."

"Lead on, said Fred as he thought, "please let Rhonda and Paul and Red be awake and watching."

Walking down Clement Street
Shuffling both my nervous feet.
Hoping that I have a fate
Better than some well-hooked bait.

Fred walked out of the bookstore. Across the street, Fred's trio of friends watched as Fred, Ferret, and Mr. Phrenology continued up Clement.

"That guy leading Fred really does look like a ferret. The

one behind looks like a human dumbbell. This must be the real thing. We are in code red," Paul said as he started out the door, but Rhonda stepped in front of him.

"They won't suspect a woman as much. I'll go. You stay back a bit with the bike and, Red, you're our base. Stay here with the coffee. We'll report back when we find out where they're heading."

"Yes, General Ma'am." Red saluted and chawed his tobacco.

Rhonda followed a block back behind Fred and his new friends. They walked through one or two commercial blocks and stopped at Busvan. Ferret held the door open for Fred. Rhonda waited. Paul coasted on the bike and caught up to her.

"They're trying to lose anyone following. This place has exits everywhere. Go check the back. I'll cover the front."

Paul pedaled down the street, turned the corner, and saw a loading dock. Behind it a white delivery van waited. Phrenology pushed Fred into the back and jumped in to drive. Ferret followed grabbing the shotgun seat. The van pulled out; the chase was on.

They turned and headed toward the Presidio. This was a mistake because everything was downhill from there and gravity gave a lot of horsepower to Paul's bicycle. He took the fast long dip through the Army base and ended up near the Veterans' Pet Cemetery. He passed the Vets Hospital and raced out the gate into the Marina behind the van. A half block and the van pulled into a driveway, stopped, opened a garage door, and drove in. Paul cruised by and went to the corner to watch. This was it. Bomber HQ. Now back for the Red and Rhonda rescue team, but first he checked for a spot they could hide in when they returned. Back behind the gates for the Presidio, behind the wall, under the bushes, they could spy on the house. But first he had the climb back up through the base, back to Clement Street to find his two friends.

Fred was as comfortable as possible for someone sitting on the floor of the van with a bandana tied around his eyes. He leaned against the wall and slid sideways with each turn. No one spoke. They rode ten minutes. When the doors opened, they were in the basement garage of an old wooden house—Fred could see the two by fours and the old plumbing pipes. Maybe a Victorian, he thought, but that was no help to Fred trying to figure out where he was. In San Francisco, Victorian houses were everywhere.

Phrenology tightened the bandana around Fred's head.

"OK, Mister friend of the Revolution, climb the stairs, keep the bandana tight," Ferret said.

The three clomped upwards. Fred tripping and grabbing the wall.

"They must have the whole house to make this much noise. More voices. A woman. Another man or two." Fred thought as he counted five of them.

"Got him. We keep him on ice until we get the book," Ferret called out.

Fred was pushed to another stairway and up and finally into a bathroom. Ferret pulled down Fred's bandana.

"Just rest. There's reading material. We'll let you go, but first you get the notebook."

Fred played it straight. "My friend has it. I can't phone

him because the cops may be listening. I do a call into KSAN on the morning show and give a place and time in the dedication. Then it's showtime with the book. Then it's yours. I want to get it to you. I'm on your side."

Fred was getting better at lying. He was not thinking revolutionary thoughts. He was on his own side, no one else's. That's what he was thinking. His side and Rhonda's and Paul's and Red's too. But he was faking the revolution with these guys.

"We get the book first, then we give you the Patty Hearst test."

Fred caught his breath. He remembered Patty got kidnapped and then joined her kidnappers. And robbed a bank. And didn't she shoot someone? Or maybe at someone? Or maybe she just made some gun noise. "Bang Bang. I'll have to rob a bank? Then the FBI will love me," Fred thought.

Ferret had Fred strip, took his clothes and wallet, and gave him a pair of pajamas that must have come from Mr. Phrenology. They were big enough for two Freds, and Fred was not a little guy.

"Rest well. We get the notebook tomorrow. And you had better hope that your KSAN plan works. Today rest. Enjoy. The tub—it's an antique clawfoot—works as a bed, a bit firm but we'll bring pillows, and you have a great white throne to sit upon and think about life. There's reading material, 'Marxism Today.' Study hard. You'll get a test in the morning to see if you can join our merry band. And we'll bring you food later. Be comfortable. You are now a semi-official, probationary part of the revolution."

Ferret closed the door. Fred heard a key turning in the

old, large keyholes, the type that Victorian San Francisco houses had in every room. Then a big piece of furniture, maybe a dresser, was slid against the door.

The window was tiny. The door secure. Fred was locked in for the night.

"He's in there." Paul pointed through the underbrush at the house where he had seen the van turn in.

"And we're out here. What do we do?" Rhonda asked.

"I think watch until we see how many there are. If they're all like that gorilla with the shaved head who was with the ferret face—yep, he did look like a ferret—then we need reinforcements. Maybe we call the Trots and Maoists over."

"You're forgetting the prime directive—don't get Fred killed," Rhonda said. "You're right, Paul. We watch."

Red scratched his chin. "I figure you two can watch well enough. I'm going to go get some dinner down that way and come back soon. You two want anything?"

SUNDAY

Sunday Morning

> *Slept so well inside the tub*
> *Por-ce-lain was quite the rub,*
> *Rubbed my leg and rubbed my head*
> *My foot's asleep, My brain is dead.*

"OK, let's get the notebook."

Ferret had opened the door to the bathroom. Phrenology backed him up.

"What's this code of yours to get it?"

"Where do you want to pick up the book? And when?"

"Palace of Fine Arts. Anyplace near there. About noon."

Fred rummaged through his brain for some street names for the message. His walks had not been in vain. He remembered walking Baker Street and crossing Beach and seeing the Palace across the lawn.

"Dedicate a song to Baker Beach—Beach and Baker Streets—that corner is right in front of the Place And make the song "Twelve Thirty" –close enough to noon, right? —by the Mamas and Papas, I think. My friend will show but will be expecting me."

"It'll have to do. You're here until we get the book."

The door closed, the key turned, and the dresser slid back. Fred heard talking downstairs. Someone started singing Mamas and Papas hits. Poor Mama Cass. All dead. Maybe I'll get to join her. They didn't sound very convinced I was a true convert to their way of thinking.

> *I would like to live a bunch*
> *But sometimes I get me a hunch*
> *My number's up, my time is done,*
> *My future, it don't look like fun.*

Fred leaned back in the tub to contemplate his fate and read back issues of *Marxism Today*, in case there was a test.

A door slammed downstairs. Fred tried the window. It was painted shut and his head wouldn't fit through anyway. He banged the walls and ceiling. Solid. He jiggled the door. Someone came up the stairs.

"What d'you want?" Why're you making noise?"

It was a new voice.

"You got any breakfast?"

"What the hell. Come on down."

A little guy opened the door.

He was short but wore some kind of muscle shirt letting him bulge out of the armpits His hair bristled, his mustache, too.

"You're going with us anyway so why not see us. And I'm a black belt so no screwing around. Lisa down here is too."

"Go with you, where?" Fred asked as he followed the bristly-headed muscle man down the steps.

"Surprise."

"I studied your Marxism magazine. Ask me anything?"

"Here's the big question: why the hell do you have our Lab notebook?"

"I was trying to help. Mr. Ferret—that's what I call him—he dropped it. In the fire. In the explosion in the lab. I was behind him trying to escape, and I'm just trying to return it." Fred looked at the three faces watching him at the foot of the stairs. "And join up with you to start the revolution."

"Mr. Ferret—gotta remember that. Our chief revolutionary brain is a ferret." Bristles looked at his fellow conspirators and gave a loud laugh. "Come on and eat your revolutionary breakfast. And I ought to finish packing."

Fred saw bags by the door. Some were already stuffed.

"Have some Wheaties. And some peaches." Lisa said, her long curly red hair poking out like Orphan Annie as she poured a few peaches from the quart can on the table into his bowl. "Sorry no first-class service in this hotel. We're in a hurry. You want milk, find a cow."

This matched Fred's style of eating—function over style. The way a field army or a teenage kid might do it. Fred felt accepted by these three. They didn't seem to care what he did. He wondered about heading for the door but remembered the muscles on the bristly one. And the supposed black belts for him and curly Lisa. Number three was fat. He didn't look like much of a problem until Fred saw the pistol lying on the table. Fred would eat his Wheaties and stay quiet.

"Now you aren't going to be a problem, are you?" the fat one asked.

"Me, a problem? I'm a born-again revolutionary."

"Well, don't get carried away. Edward—you call him Ferret—is the uptight born-again one in the group. He runs things and writes the rules: no dope, no nothing, except when he's gone. Got anything on you?"

"Come on, Jimmy. Today of all days. No screwing around." Lisa gave the fat one the evil eye. "And Fred, if you have any dope, flush it. Where we're going it's frowned upon."

"They have fine stuff in Cuba, I hear," Jimmy smiled at Fred sensing a fellow traveler from the marijuana fields.

"Just cool it. We have all day to wait and don't need this," Mr. Bristles spoke like he was in command. At least until ferret-faced Edward came home.

"When's the flight leave, anyway?" Jimmy asked. "I need a wide seat, no window, no center. I won't fit in anywhere but aisle."

"Don't worry we've got lots of time to work out seating," Lisa replied.

Fred moved to an easy chair. The three revolutionaries sat in the living room looking at each other. Bristly was nervous. Jimmy was eating chips. Lisa, the calmest of the group, kept her eye on Fred."

"So you want to join the revolution.?" she asked.

Maybe this was his test.

"I want to cut the balls off the capitalistic war mongers,

trim the sails of the imperialist running dogs, banish the bourgeois bigots." Fred felt like he covered his bases.

"And that's why you smell like a whorehouse?" Lisa shook her head when she spoke.

"I have a skin problem and use several herbal ointments." Fred didn't want to go into detail about his incense-making connection.

"You smell like you roll in patchouli oil and who knows what. I might have to lock you up in the bathroom again just to get rid of the smell down here."

"You get used to it. My girlfriend says that. Well sometimes she says that when she's in a good mood."

"OK, you're now a part of the Summer Soldiers—we'll show you the secret handshake. But first we need you to clean off that smell."

Fred figured they were keeping six eyes on him, too many for comfort, too many for him to make an escape. Maybe it would ease up on the way to the plane trip to Cuba. He needed to get away before that happened. The only flight was on Skyjacker Airlines and that would get his face on even more wanted posters. But he saw Bristles and Lisa watching him. He would play newbie revolutionary for now.

"How about sharing the chips, Jimmy? And give me some clean clothes and I'll wash up and get rid of the smell. I'm about Jimmy's size." Well maybe half, Fred thought, but they don't want me to smell like an incense factory, so I'll clean. up "I'm heading for the tub. I'll smell better, I promise."

Splashing, splashing in the tub
Doing an ungodly scrub
Taking off some skin and smell
Ready to fly off to hell.

Or maybe Cuba.

Fred came down the steps wrapped in a blanket. "Got them clean clothes for me?"

"Later. For now, you can play Lady Godiva off her high horse—makes it easier to watch out for you. Edward the Ferret will like you looking like a blanket taco. Better than chaining you to the stairs like he wanted to do. Isn't that right, Mr. Fred Arnold of Capp Street, San Francisco."

Bristles held up Fred's wallet as he spoke.

"You know me, now how about you? We haven't been introduced."

"I'm Eric, my *nom de guerre*. And now I'll do you a favor and get rid of your ID. Fred is no more. Fred is dead." He threw the wallet in the trash.

"Glad to meet you, Eric. Glad to be dead. Now can I have some clothes.?"

"Edward is coming back so we need him to see us in control. No clothes is control. Edward likes that sort of thing. Everything by the book. Damn scientist types."

Fred sashayed over to the easy chair and sat. Lisa laughed.

"Tomorrow things will be better. We'll be drinking rum and Cuba-cola and dancing all night. And don't you tell Edward anything about Cuba, Fred. He likes to keep our secrets quiet."

Fred was thinking of a way out, "These three are awful loosey-goosey for being bomb-brained revolutionaries. Bristles/Eric is filling one of the bags, Jimmy is heavily involved with peanut butter, and Lisa is reading some timetable, I should just get up and walk out and see what they do."

Fred stood and stretched. Lisa and Eric started talking. The gun was out of sight. Jimmy was spreading peanut butter on crackers. Fred sauntered around the room and hitched up his blanket. He figured he could drop all pretenses of being on their side, drop the blanket, and run out the door. He got close to the front entrance and then in one quick move grabbed the handle, threw the door open, let go of the blanket, and ran.

If anyone saw him and his pink, well-scrubbed skin, they would call the cops to get this crazy off the streets. That's what Fred wanted. Cops. He ran down the sidewalk toward Lombard Street. Traffic was always a mess there, and some cop would have him in a headlock in two seconds. Eric was a hundred yards back. Fred panted but running naked and barefoot on smooth concrete had some advantages. No clothes to slow. No shoes to weigh down his feet. But Eric was in good shape, so he was gaining.

An older gentleman wearing a blazer, grey wool slacks, and a fedora raised his walking stick and started yelling at Fred. "Damn hippies, go back to the Haight and stay there, or I'm going to call the cops."

"Come on, Pops, call them cops," Fred yelled as he picked up his pace. His body and associated parts bounced up and down, and the old man looked away.

Then a van pulled around the corner. After a second when the driver was figuring out the situation, it aimed at Fred, who cut around the driver's side to get away, but the van skidded to a half-stop, and Mr. Phrenology, all one-eighth ton of him, jumped out with the van still moving, grabbed Fred, and threw him in over top of the driver's seat. Fred fell next to something soft.

"Hi, Fred."

It was Rhonda.

Sunday Afternoon

Rhonda sat on the throne, Fred on the edge of the tub. Fred was naked; Rhonda wore her usual jeans and wool shirt. The bathroom door had been locked after they were shoved in. The dresser pushed back in place. Yelling was happening downstairs. Ferrety Edward was not big but had a big voice. Eric, Lisa, and Jimmy kept quiet. Phrenology chimed in every so and so. He had a squeaky voice for someone so large. Maybe that was why he beefed up.

"You call yourselves revolutionaries. You let our target escape. Did he signal anyone? Tell me what happened," Edward the Ferret ranted loud enough for the two upstairs to hear.

Lisa was the only one brave enough to answer. "We brought Fred down here. He was going to see us anyway, so we fed him, but we took his clothes so he couldn't get away, but he ran anyway. We watched him the whole time—no signaling, who could he signal anyway, unless he did it by wiggling his ass. You got the notebook, right? So all is set? No harm, no foul."

Rhonda moved next to Fred on the tub edge and started whispering. "Red and Paul are in the van watching. He picked up the van from the incense factory last night to follow these guys."

"But he doesn't have a key for it."

"Creative wiring. It's a Volkswagen—they were built for that. But the big news is Red and I burned the notebook. In a barbecue pit on the Presidio. We had marshmallows and hotdogs with it last night. Paul stood watch over your friend Ferret's house, and we brought Paul a hot wiener special."

"So how'd you get caught?"

"I met them at the KSAN spot—Beach and Baker. I listened to the radio while we were watching the house. Their van showed up at noon and Phrenology didn't say anything. He just scooped me up and stuck me in the back. Then I told them the notebook was cooked, fried, toasted. They threatened me, but I said I burned it, because when you disappeared, I got scared. I think they believed me They saw the ashes on my shirt. I smell like a campfire."

"What do we do?"

"Well, Paul thinks we should wait until some of them leave or they take us away. Red wants a frontal attack."

"It's got to be quick. They're off to Cuba. Tonight. And no flights except hijacked ones go there. And they have guns— well, at least one. And their suitcases are almost packed. Who knows if they have bombs. We need to figure something out."

The dresser slid away from in front of the bathroom door and the key turned. The door opened. Edward the Ferret stood looking at them.

Fred started the introductions "Rhonda this is the brains, who we call The Ferret, his name is Edward, but that's probably a fake name, his *nom de guerre*."

"Nice to meet you, Edward." Rhonda extended her right hand ready to shake.

"My name is Edward. Remember that! Downstairs now."

The Ferret passed Fred a blanket that he wrapped tight around himself. He followed Rhonda and Edward; Phrenology brought up the rear.

"Everyone at the table!" Edward was in command mode.

Fred and Rhonda got the hot seats, in the middle where everyone watched them. The Ferret started the inquisition.

"You said you wanted to join, but you ran. You said you wanted to give me the notebook, but your friend says she burned it. How can I believe anything? How can I not believe you're infiltrators? CIA spooks? Traitors to the cause?"

Fred blurted, "I heard Jimmy talk about Cuba and got scared. That's why I ran."

The Ferret eyeballed Jimmy like the fat man was the weak link in a sausage factory, like he would give away secret after secret for something tasty.

"I'm a San Francisco boy, a Berkeleyite—I don't want to leave. So I ran. But I still want to join the revolution. But I want to do it here. I'm with you guys. But I'm a homeboy."

Rhonda chimed in, "I was scared too. No wonder I burned the book after you kidnapped Fred. I know you have to be secret, but you just took him with no word. Then I got scared about the notebook. I didn't know what you'd do, so I threw it in a fireplace. Then I got the message on the KSAN that you sent and showed up, and you treated me like some fascist pig."

Rhonda spit out the word pig. She was good at this. She would make a real sparkplug for the revolution.

The Ferret gave them a long look, then smiled. "I can reconstruct the notebook. It's in my head, so we'll be OK. Just need to bargain more when we land. And about the flight, the good news is you two will get a chance to prove yourselves tonight. You will get pistols to take onboard the plane, and you will hijack the plane while we critique. If you're good, then one day we shall give you real weapons." He chuckled and looked closely at Fred. "One day in Cuba when you are cutting sugar cane, we will start you out on machetes. But don't worry—we'll be sitting in the plane near you tonight, carrying weapons that can punch big holes in people, blow them into little pieces, in case you have problems. Or are one."

"Us two, do the hijacking? I don't know one end of a pistol from the other." Fred was lying—he had banged away with a forty-five when he was in the army.

"Nothing to it. Just stick the barrel in the ribs of a stewardess and hand her a note in the back galley. Tell her to call the pilot on the intercom. The note will give directions for flying to Havana. I'll write it for you. Then sit down with the stewardess, hold the gun on her, and enjoy the flight.

"And me? Do I have to do it too?" Rhonda asked.

"You go up front with the pilot and hold your gun on him. Tell him your luggage is filled with bombs, so he must do what you say or kaput. A big kaput up in the sky. Just open the door to the cockpit and walk in with a big smile and the barrel sticking out of your jacket. Tell the copilot to move and sit in his seat. Lisa and I will be in the front row and greet the copilot with our little bullet spitting friends. My big friend will be in the back, watching Fred. Eric will be watching the passengers. Having you two makes our life easier. We can monitor what's going on much better if you take the lead."

"Happy to help." Rhonda tried to sound enthusiastic.

"Lisa will give you both jogging suits, so you don't stand

out, and Jimmy will get you guns. Eric will show you what to do. But there is no rush. The Midnight Flyer leaves at—well what do you know—Midnight."

"Finally, to make sure you don't get any counterrevolutionary ideas, we ask you to sit on the stairs where we can see you. Welcome to the revolution."

> *I've got a feeling not so dandy*
> *'bout flying with this crazy band-y.*
> *We will make a big news splash*
> *And maybe do a nose-first crash.*
> *But I'd rather to old Cuba go*
> *and do a wheels-down land-y-o.*

Rhonda bent forward and whispered to Fred. "Come on, it's not that bad. We're alive and together, and probably going to sunny Cuba. You like warm places. And we're not part of the gang—really, we're not. We'll get back. And clear our names. And get out of jail someday."

One bike lock secured her wrist to the railing on the stairs. Another held Fred sitting three steps down.

"We're going to die and get locked up in jail for a thousand years. And the electric chair, too."

"Remember, Paul and Red are nearby."

"Do they know anything about us going to Cuba? How are they going to help?"

"They're smart and clever and there for us."

Sunday 9 p.m.

"T-time for the Summer Soldiers," The Ferret called out as he looked at his watch. "Checklist."

"Manifestos? "Ready."

Fred looked at Rhonda and mouthed, "manifestos?"

"Guns?" "Ready."

"Hostages?" "Ready."

"Hostage weapons?"

"Ready as hell." Fred called out. Both he and Rhonda held up their guns—kids' cap guns, with "Roy Rogers" emblazoned across their fake pearl handles. They stood in their new jogging suits—courtesy of Lisa's quick run to the sports shop—next to Phrenology who kept a tight eye on them.

"You called us hostages? I thought we were part of the freedom fighters for the revolution?" Rhonda leaned forward with her hands on her hips staring straight at Edward.

"You're part of the Summer Soldiers. But, let us say, on a trial membership, like when you join a record club. And remember your gun is as good as any other. It's fear we want to spread, not bullets."

"Well, I sure don't have any bullets," Fred laughed nervously waving his cap gun in the air. "What do I do? Say, 'Bang, Bang, you're dead.'"

"They were all I could find," Jimmy said looking down and shaking his head. "They look real enough. If you cover up the pearl handles."

"You want me to hijack a plane with a toy gun.'"

"Just hold the barrel against their back. No one will know the difference if you're close. And tell them about the bombs in the luggage. They'll do what you say. They've had training in this type of situation to go with the flow as they say these days. And we're your backup." The Ferret stuck his gun into Fred's ribs. "Do it like this. See, you couldn't tell if it was a pistol or a hash pipe. Easy as pie."

> *Summer Soldiers on the go*
> *Plotting now to start the show*
> *Got my pop gun—that thing's hot*
> *I just hope I don't get shot*

Edward and Lisa sat in the front of the van with the others perched in back on luggage or sitting on the floor. Fred held his toy gun in his lap until Rhonda told him to stuff it into his jacket as she had. The others had their pistols tucked away.

"Not every day you hijack a plane. We should probably get Summer Soldier T-shirts to wear." Fred was trying small talk as they rode down the peninsula toward the airport.

"Keep them quiet back there," Edmond the Ferret yelled. Phrenology made a zipper motion across his lips looking at Fred.

The airport was not crowded at 11 p.m. on Saturday night except at the PSA counter. A line of customers wove around rows of seats as two hundred or so stood waiting to buy tickets on this, the cheapest of all flights. You could wing it to LA for $11.75 standby or pay the full thirteen bucks to be sure of getting a seat. The only rule was no checked baggage, nothing but carry-on, so everyone planned for a fight to get space in the overheads when they boarded.

Fred wondered how any airline could charge so little, but PSA was the upstart: cheap flights, day-glow pink miniskirted stews revealing more than they covered, pink and orange striped planes, pilots doing standup over the loudspeaker instead of altitude and weather reports, and a big goofy smile painted on every airplane's nose. PSA fit into a hang-loose, West Coast vibe, making a go of goofiness. Just the plane to take on an unscheduled flight to Havana.

Two thirds of the waiting line were longhairs heading to LA beaches and warmer places than San Francisco could provide; a few were down-and-outs; one group, however, looked like it was on the wrong plane, carrying helmets and backpacks and wearing matching jumpsuits with "Sky Cruisers" embroidered across the back; the rest of the line just looked confused.

Most sat on the floor after getting their boarding passes. Some strummed guitars and sang folk songs; a few earnestly read thick, dog-eared books; a dozen napped; some smoked; and some went into the restrooms and smoked something stronger. Babies dawdled on the floor. Only a dozen frolicking dogs were needed to make this scene rival the hippieness of Golden Gate Park.

The ticket clerks looked on, bemused, thinking back to their old days when college kids wore blazers and bobby sox and considered it exciting to stuff themselves into a phone booth.

The hijackers sat together: Fred on one of their bags after checking for any wires or bulges that might explode. Rhonda was next to him, against the wall.

"Keep the Ferret busy, I see something at the counter," she whispered.

Fred looked at Edward—he tried not to think of him as the Ferret, afraid he might call him that and he didn't want to set him off.

Fred started a rapid-fire distraction. "Don't they check us? Will we get on? Anything I should do to get ready?"

"Just smile. Don't attract attention. We don't quite fit in—a bit upscale for this group—but I've been here at the airport twice to see how it works. No one checks anything. They just make hippy jokes and herd you like doped-up sheep."

Rhonda gave Fred a nudge and a nod in the direction of the check-in desk. Red and Paul stood in front of the counter buying tickets.

"I see you can smoke on these things, but how about a tobacco chaw." Red said with enough volume to overcome the chorus of Kumbaya by the folk singers. He stared at Fred and winked.

Paul fumbled in his pocket for the twenty-six dollars and realized he forgot his wallet in the car.

"Your IDs please?"

"Crap, I gotta run back to the car. You hold our place in line, Red."

"What line? This here's a herd not a line?"

"Our rescue team has arrived." Rhonda muttered.

Fred walked slowly through the door held open by the flight assistant and started down the outdoor stairway out of the terminal while looking back at the line. Red and Paul were far in the back. Ferret gave him a nudge.

"We don't have all night."

Fred and Rhonda reached the bottom of the stairs. Fred thought about running, but Phrenology was an arm's reach away. The plane was twenty yards out from the terminal, attended to by a truck pumping gas and a mechanic looking at the front landing gear. There was nothing but open space, nowhere to go.

"Maybe it won't take off. Maybe it has a broken landing-gear, or a sick pilot, and they'll call it off," Fred's mind churned out scenarios, all hopeful to start with but ending with him in prison, dead, and alone.

Flying south on PSA
Hopeful of another day
When sunshine rules and happiness
Smiles on me and clears this mess.

Fred, Rhonda and the Summer Soldier Five walked at the front of the line of passengers crossing the tarmac, passing under the plane's nose with its big painted grin. One pilot looked down from the cockpit, leaning out an open side window to see how boarding was going. Fred walked under the wing and passed to the rear of the plane where a ramp had been lowered from the back of the fuselage. It trembled and bounced as Fred and Rhonda climbed. Phrenology and Lisa climbed aboard behind them. The others had gone ahead and were stashing their bags. Lisa gave Rhonda a push toward the front.

Ferret and Fred took seats in the back row where Fred looked out the window and saw Paul waving his arms up and down, standing behind the large glass windowpanes of the terminal. The exit door in the terminal had closed, and he and Red were left behind.

> *We are screwed and we are stuck*
> *We're just a pair of seated ducks*
> *Our rescuers are standing tall*
> *Locked in the airport's takeoff hall*
> *No one's gonna save our skins*
> *'specially our landlocked friends.*

"Welcome aboard. This is section one of the Midnight Special, your late-night, short-haul, long-hair adventure. If some of you have friends that didn't make it on this plane, another section of the flight will be boarding in twenty minutes. You can meet up in LA."

Paul and Red were going to get the next plane. "Maybe we meet up in Cuba," Fred thought. He didn't know if Rhonda knew they were alone on the plane, alone with five hijackers, one hundred thirty passengers, seven crew members, and a bomb or two. But no Paul or Red.

One of the pilots, wearing a wig and a poncho stuck his head out the cockpit door. "If you see smoke from the cockpit, don't worry we're just trying to get high, I mean gain altitude."

The passengers laughed. The Midnight Special often felt like tryouts for a comedy hour.

"Remember no smoking until we get off the ground."

The hijackers hadn't laughed. Fred stared straight ahead. His brain was empty. His life was over. At least his get-out-of-jail-free, San Francisco life.

"Close those doors and we'll be off."

Fred sat in the aisle seat in the last row with Edward the Ferret beside him. Rhonda was somewhere in the front. She was too short for Fred to see, but Phrenology's head bobbed up near the door to the cockpit. Fred figured he was keeping a tight rein on Rhonda. The other three hijackers were scattered around the plane. A stewardess walked by giving a tug on Fred's seatbelt and smiling at The Ferret.

"Prepare for takeoff," the pilot announced over the loudspeaker. "Remember smoking is only allowed for tobacco, except in international airspace." After a short pause he added, "and California is as spacy as you get."

A few passengers smiled at the attempted joke. Fred studied his knees and squeezed the toy gun in his pocket.

The plane lifted off, and then after a few minutes the seat belt and no smoking signs went dark. A stewardess came to the back and started to pull out a rolling cart. The Ferret nudged Fred, "Show time."

"OK, folks, we have a slight change of plans. A gentleman in the back of the plane has asked us to make a short diversion to Havana, so off we go. We'll refuel in one hour and then play hopscotch across the US until we get to Cuba. I asked our friend to let most of you off the plane. Ten hostages are as good as a hundred, I believe, so we'll see what he says. Now have a comfortable flight. And don't worry. This is PSA, the airline with a smile."

Airplane crews had been trained to go along with hijackers. And believe them if they said they had a bomb. The FBI would catch the bad guys later. The immediate goal was to get everyone down safely, and, of course, the airline wouldn't mind getting its plane back in working order.

Rhonda was standing behind the pilots. Phrenology stood behind her and held his pistol toward her back. He wasn't as trusting as the Ferret about the two new additions to the team. And he definitely didn't trust the pilots.

Eric also was standing and had moved up to the front of the cabin. He grabbed the microphone from the stewardess.

"Everyone put your hands on the seat in front of you where we can see them. We plan on everyone being safe, so help us and keep quiet. And stewardess, turn the cabin lights on."

Eric was counting all the clinched fingers grabbing the seatbacks. A few hands were missing.

"I said everyone with their hands on the seat."

"You come hold my baby then," a voice called out from mid-plane.

The flight had settled down, much of California had passed under the wings as they approached LA. Phrenology gave the pilot orders to drop to two thousand feet and slow to one hundred and fifty knots. Flaps down.

"You said I was going to highjack the plane and now you're taking over." Rhonda looked at Phrenology.

"Get in the back and stash your gun."

"Sure, it did me a lot of good."

Rhonda dropped it. The toy gun bounced in the aisle. One of the stewardesses standing in the aisle laughed when she saw Roy Rogers name on the handle.

"You been demoted girl," the stewardess said.

"I got hijacked too. Didn't you see, it's a toy gun. The ferret-faced guy made us do this," Rhonda whispered as she passed the stewardess.

"You two, help me here. Pull down these bags," The Ferret called out to Fred and Rhonda.

The overhead bins were stuffed. Fred pulled down a half-dozen bags before he got the ones that the Ferret wanted. Rhonda stacked the others in the aisle.

"Take those two bags and go to the back of the plane. Your job is to distribute our manifestos to Los Angeles."

"This guy is one whacko. How do I distribute manifestos up here?" thought Fred as he picked up two bags and carried them to the back of the galley.

"Pilot, keep level at two thousand. And circle downtown LA."

Air whooshed in when the plane depressurized, and passengers yawned to pop their ears. Fred banged on the side of his head. Rhonda stared at The Ferret.

"Pull that lever and walk down the ramp," he yelled.

Fred pulled. The boarding ramp lowered itself behind

the rear galley and locked into place.

"Walk down the ramp? I don't leave this place until we're on the ground," Fred said as he looked at Rhonda and shook his head. "It just leads to fresh air."

She turned her back to The Ferret, mouthing words, "Play along. We're OK. But hold tight to the rail."

The ramp was blocked. The back of the galley was lined with backpacks, all the same, all with "Sky Cruisers" stenciled across them.

"Move the backpacks. Throw them down the stairs. Get down there and start tossing out our manifestos. Pull them out of our bags," The Ferret yelled over the noise of the wind whistling around the ramp.

Fred and Rhonda moved to the first steps and saw Los Angeles passing below the bottom step.

"We are not thugs, not criminals. We are angry. We are incensed at what is happening. We are changing the world. Our manifesto explains it to the workers. Start scattering them on Los Angeles. Do it."

"Wasn't your Manifesto printed in the Times already? Isn't that enough?" Rhonda looked back at Ferret who was about to give a speech to the passengers.

"The proletariat doesn't read the Times."

"They don't read anything; they watch TV," she mumbled. "You should've hijacked a skywriter plane."

Rhonda grabbed one of the backpacks with the Sky Cruiser logos to move it out of the way. "Fred, these things are parachutes. That group must be some kind of jumping club," she yelled into Fred's ear.

She walked down the ramp with Fred holding on to her and the railing. Fred carried the bag filled with the Sunshine Soldiers' precious manifestos.

"You do the dump; I'll be your anchor," Fred called out as he interlocked hands with her.

Rhonda opened one of the bags and poured leaflets into the churning air. It looked like a New Year's parade full of tickertape and fluttering paper for a moment. Then the paper cloud sailed farther and farther behind. She turned to Fred and started back up the ramp, holding on to his hand and the railing.

Fred stayed on the ramp while Rhonda went for the next bag. She also grabbed two of the backpack parachutes that had fallen partway down the ramp. The Ferret had turned toward the passengers and was explaining capitalism and unemployment to a crowd that wanted nothing more than communes, dope, and free love. A few were more politically inclined, and one young bearded man started chanting, "Ho Ho Ho Chi Minh. On to Cuba; goin' to win." Most just wanted to get themselves on the ground, off the plane, and into something safe and comfortable.

"Let's get out of here. No one can see us. Help me put this thing on," Rhonda yelled into Fred's ear.

Fred knew parachutes—he had jumped in the army. He grabbed Rhonda. "Wait, we're over a city. We don't know anything about these chutes. You don't just put on any one of these like you would a pair of pajamas."

"I know a way out when I see it. We bail and then we tell them we were kidnapped. You'll be a free boy."

Fred thought for a second. Rhonda started strapping the chute to her back.

"How does this damn thing work anyway? You coming?"

Fred landed in a field; Rhonda on a school lawn a half mile away. She twisted her ankle; Fred lucked out and bounced on soft turf. He pulled off the parachute and ran to the road. He had seen where Rhonda came down and ran toward her but slowed and started waving his arms when a long black Lincoln came up the road. It pulled over.

"That was some stunt jumping out of an airliner. You a stuntman or something?"

"I got kidnapped by some crazies and escaped. My ladyfriend landed over there. Take me there, please."

Sirens were faint but getting louder. Someone had seen them coming down and called the cops. They started off in the direction toward where Rhonda had landed."

"Well, buddy, how'd you ever get out of a flying airliner. Don't they lock the doors?"

"727s got a ramp in the back. We climbed out on it to escape. Help me find Rhonda. She's over here somewhere."

Rhonda came limping toward them. Fred jumped out of the car, ran, and grabbed her.

"We did it. We're alive," Fred yelled as he spun Rhonda.

"Go easy. I've got a bum ankle."

Fred helped Rhonda into the front seat of the Lincoln.

"Can you take us someplace where we can just sit and rest."

"Sure ma'am. You two jumped out of a 727." The driver gave his two passengers a long look. "I can't believe that."

"You better. Some guys with guns kidnapped us and hijacked the plane buy we got away." Rhonda was rehearsing her story for the cops.

"I'll drop you two here in the park. I'm late, so you have a nice day."

"Thanks, man. What did you say your name was? I want to give you lots of credit when the cops get here"

"Just call me Dan, Dan B. Cooper. But keep me out of this, OK? The cops and I don't get along too well."

Sirens were getting closer as the Lincoln drove away. Fred and Rhonda hugged tight. A Summer Soldier flyer landed on the ground near their feet. Dan drove away looking up at the sky, smiling at the 727 still circling in the clouds.

You reach the end and you survived,
All your friends are still alive,
You got a tale for the FBI
'Bout getting hijacked in the sky,
And Rhonda's standing at your side
And breakfast's ready to be fried
With eggs and donuts on the side

ABOUT THE AUTHOR

Charles Kerns writes mysteries about life in San Francisco and Oaxaca, Mexico (see his *Santo Gordo Mysteries*). He lives in Oakland, California with his wife Roshni, his bicycle, and a collection of international mysteries.

I conflated many events of those years into the time span of this book. It did feel as though everything happened that quickly back then. All the characters are imagined, the places mostly real, the foods, unfortunately, were real, and the events about 50/50.

If the book were more real, then this would be a history book, not a mystery.

Made in the USA
Las Vegas, NV
04 August 2022